ROBBIE

ROBBIE

or How to be a Detective

Caroline Conran

UNIVERSE

Contents

CHAPTER 1

Vanishing trick

I am Robbie. I don't have any brothers or sisters. It's just me. I live in Northern Ireland, in a town called Arlen. My parents are always annoying me with their arguing. They even row about what we have for breakfast. Mum hates cooking, so that's when it starts – at breakfast.

I don't want to hear it, so I go to my secret place in the woods, on the far side of the field at the back, and look for spies.

I want to catch a spy and put handcuffs on him. Then I'll have him at my mercy. I'll bring sandwiches and eat them in front of him one by one, until he's so hungry he tells me everything.

My school is near my house and I can get there on my bike. I'll chain the spy to the railings of the school and everyone will say, 'Robbie caught that villain!' and then I'll feel like a real detective, which is what I want to be.

Arlen is a ferry port, and my dad's the ferry master and he's an Orangeman. He's called Mark. He wears a bowler hat and marches with his friends. He's very strict and he quotes the Bible – a lot. My mum is called Rosanna but everyone calls her Rose. She sometimes works at the health centre but she's mostly at home. She looks out for me when Dad is in a bad mood.

My parents row about everything. For instance, who should have the car, what time meals are, and whether I should have braces on my teeth. Mum won that one in the end, but Dad thought it was all vanity. I don't mind the braces very much. Not if it means I'm going to look more like Robbie Williams, who I think I was named after.

Upstairs in my room I play his music quite loud through my headphones so I don't have to listen to the slamming doors and shouting coming from the kitchen. Sometimes I can hear my mother throwing pans on the floor. Dad doesn't want her to sing, and that makes her dead angry. Sometimes she breaks things. I have to pretend not to be there, to be invisible. It's very useful for a detective to be able to hide.

I chose a good hiding place under a tree in the woods behind the house. I feel invisible when I'm there, but I can see the house. I can see what's going on.

I want a pair of binoculars for Christmas. I said I want them for birdwatching but it's really for watching people and finding things out.

I'm going for a bike ride in a moment. My mum seems quite pleased. I'll go up there and cover my bike in the leaves and then I will hide.

I'm wearing my fleece, which is warm, and I've put some biscuits in my pocket in case I have to stay there a long time. After all, detectives often have to watch for hours and hours.

I'm lying in the leaves under my tree. I'm watching the windows of my house. If anyone finds me I'll say I'm birdwatching. It's not exactly a fib because I have actually seen a robin and some seagulls, although they don't count because there are hundreds of them.

It's going dark and the lights are on in the house. I can see my mum in the kitchen. She's walking up and down. I think she's waiting for someone. I can hear a car or a van or something on the road on the other side of the house. Now I can't see Mum. Oh yes, she's back and she's got a parcel. She's tearing it open. What is it? She seems very excited. It's red, bright and fluffy – like big bunches of red flowers. It looks like it might be something to wear, but no one wears red in Arlen.

I can't really see properly. It'll be better when I've got my binoculars.

Now I can hear a car. I think it's Dad coming home. Mum has disappeared out of the kitchen. She's in the living room now. I can't see the red thing anywhere. There's Dad. They look as if they're being nice to one other.

I've eaten the biscuits and I'm a bit cold. Most of the time detectives don't notice things like being cold. Maybe there'll be hot cheese-and-ham toasties for tea.

CHAPTER 2

Nobody was where they were supposed to be

Christmas Day came, and with it a bright blue sky.

'It'll freeze tonight,' said Robbie's dad.

Robbie stayed in the background as the house filled with loud, middle-aged relatives, all making stupid jokes. They wouldn't let him try the coffee with whiskey in it.

His mum gave everyone paper crowns and plates of Christmas cake and they played some silly games. Robbie found he was in luck; his main present was a good pair of birdwatcher's binoculars and a bird book.

His dad gave him a book called *Treasure Island*, about buccaneers and buried gold. He'd *really* wanted a book about detectives, but he hadn't wanted to give the game away, so he'd reluctantly left it off his list.

Robbie knew his mum was hiding something. She'd hidden the red thing, for a start. Robbie had looked all over the house, but hadn't been able to find it.

It was late afternoon but still sunny, so Robbie picked up his binoculars and called out, 'I'm just going out to try my present.'

His mum, in her blue dress, practically had her head in the

oven as she tried to baste the turkey and he could see her face was flushed red. She looked cross.

'Blasted turkey, I hate the beastly thing,' she said.

He waited impatiently.

At last she looked up from her crouching position on the floor. 'Go on then, if you're going, but don't be long. Dinner will be ready in half an hour. Mari, come and help with this blimmin' bird, will you?'

Robbie almost bumped into his aunt as she came running into the kitchen. Then he slipped quietly away.

Reaching his favourite place, he lay on his stomach in the leaves under the oak. It was bright and the air was crisp and it smelled of seaweed, woodsmoke and sump-oil.

As he became familiar with the binoculars, he started to look around, and not just at his mum's kitchen. He looked upwards. A dozen seagulls were floating above him. They looked sinister; he'd never noticed the cold yellow eyes they had.

Next he looked at the houses. Robbie's house was at the bottom of the valley and on the slope beyond were more houses, mainly painted white with grey roofs. Some had large windows and he could see a terrace or two, and some balconies.

He fiddled with the binoculars again. Now every house seemed to rush closer towards him. As he moved his gaze from left to right he could see everything in detail. Smoke rose from some of the chimneys straight up into the air. That's where the smell was coming from. He spotted a couple of large fishing nets hanging over one balcony and black wetsuits on another. Everything was outlined with soft rainbow edges. It was almost magical.

The image started to fade. Lights were coming on in the houses and fairy lights sparkled in the frosty twilight. Now, as the dusk deepened, Robbie could see into the brightly lit houses. He could see the people – they seemed close, very close, to him. He could even see the faces of the people sitting down in his own kitchen for Christmas dinner.

Christmas dinner! Half an hour, his mother had said. He'd better get back pretty fast.

He was nearly back on the road with his bike when he heard a light scrunching and a shuffle of leaves. He turned quickly. Half invisible in the gloom of the wood's edge was a dark figure creeping up on him. It suddenly jumped right at him shouting, 'Gotcha!'

It was his older cousin Jeff, Aunt Lizzie's son.

Robbie's chest shrank with fright, but he pretended it was all fine.

'Well, Robbie,' said Jeff, rather slyly, 'what might you be looking at here?'

Robbie had his answer ready. 'I'm only birdwatching, Jeff. I just saw some gulls.'

'*Birdwatching*, is it?' said Jeff.

But the way he said it made Robbie think, he knows I wasn't.

'Well, I've been sent to find you,' said Jeff, shaking his head disapprovingly, 'and here you are, up to no good. Should I call the police now, do you think?'

Robbie looked at him sharply. He was good at telling when people were angry, but Jeff was different – he looked at you straight-faced and his eyes gave nothing away.

'Hey, Jeff, you won't tell on me, will you?' he pleaded.

'Not if you let me come *birdwatching* with you next time,' said Jeff.

Robbie thought, no, I don't want you there, I want to find out about Mum's secret. Why d'you have to come and spoil everything?

But he simply said, 'OK.'

In those winter days that followed, short yet fine, Robbie took Jeff with him birdwatching. He took him to the beach, he took him to the wrong part of the woods, he took him along the road and they sat on the railway bridge for ages. Evidently Jeff, who had just left school, had nothing better to do. They were almost turning into quite good friends but then, after a few days, he simply didn't show up.

There was still New Year's Eve to come. His mum, nails polished and arms jangling with bracelets, had told Robbie and his dad at breakfast that she was going to spend the evening with Aunt Mari and would be staying overnight.

'I did my bit at Christmas,' she said, with a look at his dad that Robbie could tell meant she might start throwing things if anyone objected.

Twelve people had sat down to roast turkey, and even getting to the cooker or the plate cupboard had meant drawing in your stomach and going sideways. It was his mum who, with Aunt Mari, had done all the getting up and down, serving them all.

'Sorry, love,' the others said from time to time, 'I'd give you a hand but I can't get out.'

Robbie had seen that his mum's forehead was shiny with sweat. She'd gritted her teeth and slammed down the plates. By the time she sat down to eat, all the life had gone out of the turkey, and his mum looked the same.

And then his dad had started on at Jeff.

'When are you getting a job, boyo? You need to think about it now you've left school.'

Robbie heard his dad muttering 'waster' under his breath. Jeff was trying to avoid him by helping Robbie fill the dishwasher, when he came looming up again.

'I'll see what I can get you down at the port,' he said.

'I'm all right, thanks, Uncle Mark,' said Jeff, and he winked at Robbie. His dad walked off in a huff.

And then his mum had polished off the cranberry liqueur and started them all singing. She shut her eyes, high colour in her cheeks, and swayed to the roar of them all belting out 'Stand by Your Man'. Robbie thought she looked happy.

'Robbie can sing,' she'd said. 'He's a lovely singer.' She put her arm round his shoulders and got him to join in with her, her perfect velvety sound blending with his light, golden voice. Soon the other voices dropped away and the two of them, singing together, had held everyone spellbound in the Christmassy fug.

It's New Year's Eve. The house is horribly quiet. Mum's not here, but I can watch Dad. It will be good practice. I'm going out on my own, but I'll tell Dad I'm going birdwatching with Jeff and then he won't worry about me.

I'll take some biscuits and a can of red lemonade. I'll move Dad's special bowler hat out of the way and I can get down my old grey hoody and I'll be invisible.

Once hidden beneath the oak, Robbie wondered why his dad had said 'Is that so?' when he'd told him he was going to meet Jeff. But he didn't worry too much. He saw that the afternoon sun was slanting almost horizontally through the windows of his house, reaching the deeper parts of the sitting room where he could see his dad reading the paper. He saw someone coming in. They started talking, but his dad didn't get up. No one important, then. Seconds later, the visitor turned and Robbie recognised him with a start. Jeff! Who was supposed to be birdwatching with him! Now he was going to get a proper roasting. Jeff was pacing the room and then came to the window. He seemed to look straight at Robbie. And smiled.

I'm trying to tell what they're saying. They do look serious. Is Dad asking stuff about me? As long as he doesn't take away my binoculars, I'll be all right. I can tell Dad I changed my mind. I'm glad Jeff doesn't know about my secret place – I wonder if he does? He was looking right at me. Maybe he saw a glint from my binoculars. I think I should go undercover, move my secret place.

Now Jeff is leaving. Jeff is strange sometimes. I think I'd better keep an eye on him. No way am I going to get caught here by him, no way!

The lights are coming on. I'd better pack up. It's getting dark. My feet are cold. I wish I'd worn thick socks.

It was almost dark. The lights had gone on, and as he glanced towards the lit houses he could see figures here and there. Christmas lights still twinkled in the frosty air. As he got up, a figure in green caught his eye as it flashed about in a room behind one of the large glass windows. Like a fish in an aquarium. He fumbled for his binoculars.

He tried to focus. It was a woman in an emerald green dress. A shadowy shape appeared behind her. She was talking to someone. It was a man. He came up and put his arms round her and Robbie could clearly see his face. She turned towards the window. Who was it? There was something about her...

It was Aunt Mari! What was she doing *there* when his mother was supposed to be spending the night at her house, half a mile away?

Who was the man? Did Aunt Mari have a boyfriend? Why had she never mentioned him?

And where was his mum?

When Robbie got home, he knew he was in trouble. He tried to creep in, but his father was there waiting for him.

'Hello, son,' he said. 'Where have you been?'

'Birdwatching, Dad.'

His father laughed, but it wasn't a friendly laugh.

'Oh, so now you can see birds in the dark, can you? And I suppose you were there with Jeff?'

'No, Dad, Jeff couldn't come.' He improvised, thinking fast. His heart was pounding. His mum wasn't where she'd said she'd be and neither was Aunt Mari. Should he tell his dad?

He decided he would keep his mum's secret, which meant not telling about Aunt Mari either. He was brimming with the urge to tell someone, but who?

He could hear his dad was angry.

'Listen to me. I'm telling you – look at me – your very soul, your immortal soul, is in danger here, son. You and your tricks – it's the work of the devil himself! You know well enough about the sin of lying.'

Robbie switched off. He refused to listen and soon began to feel better. His dad was not going to take his binoculars off him, after all. He pretended to be very contrite, eyes down, fixed on the carpet. He waited for him to say, 'Now go to your room.' Those words came at last.

It was the worst New Year's Eve of his life. His mum wasn't with his aunt. There was silence in the house. No comfort anywhere. He could hear neighbours celebrating – letting the old, tarnished year go out, ready for a fresh new one, full of hope. He could hear rockets and the hiss of their flight, followed by the explosions. He got his binoculars. From his window he could see sparkling reds, greens and golds; a rush of fireworks, far away. Down below he could hear the clamour of the children next door running around with sparklers, while parents chatted.

He hadn't the heart to listen to his music. He felt deeply alone. He lay down on his bed, pulled the duvet over his head and fell asleep.

Next day, Robbie had a hasty piece of toast with chocolate spread on it and then stayed in his room with his headphones on to drown out the silence. He still felt weighed down, so big was the burden of what he knew. And it didn't seem to add up at all.

When he finally went downstairs he knew what to do. He took out his bicycle and started to cycle over to Aunt Mari's house. He was going to find out what was happening.

On his way there he went down to the docks, as he often did, and watched the morning ferry coming in. The cold air was thick and heavy with steam and oily fumes. With his binoculars he could see the faces, mainly white and strained, of the passengers.

It had probably been a late night and a rough crossing. Many would have come by coach from London on a marathon journey home for New Year's Day. And there, mingling with the passengers as they walked off the gangway and set off towards the exit, was his cousin Jeff, looking nervous. Coming off the boat was a short man in a leather jacket, who looked as if he was in a hurry. He approached Jeff. They had a quick word and the man passed something to Jeff.

Robbie quickly ran down the steps to the dock, leaving his bike on the footpath. He decided he'd better hide; a detective wouldn't want to be seen on an operation like this. He slid behind a gantry. Jeff put the object inside a rucksack and zipped it shut. Why would he do that? Surely the only explanation was that he didn't want anyone to see the package. There was something very fishy about Jeff and this man who, Robbie noticed, quickly disappeared.

Most of the passengers – dragging their luggage, shuffling their feet – went up the ramp. He lost sight of Jeff, so he went back, picked up his bike, and cycled on to his aunt's house.

Aunt Mari opened the door to Robbie and looked pleased to see him. Smiling, she welcomed him in, inviting him into the kitchen where she was in the middle of making a late breakfast. She made a plate for Robbie too – bacon and scrambled eggs. In the warm kitchen he felt safe and relaxed a bit. Aunt Mari being kind to him made him feel like crying, and a few tears leaked from his eyes, unwanted.

'What's up, love?' she said, coming round to his chair and putting her hands on his shoulders.

'I decided to be a detective,' he said. 'You know, solve crimes and discover secrets. That was what I wanted the binoculars for.'

'Not for birdwatching, then?'

'Well … that too.'

Aunt Mari took the fib in her stride.

'So what's happened?' she said.

'I need to know where Mum is.'

'Oh, she's still asleep upstairs,' said Aunt Mari.

Robbie felt bewildered. How could this be true?

But when Aunt Mari took him upstairs, Robbie's mum was fast asleep, breathing gently. Like a heap of red carnations, a dress with lots of frilly layers sat bundled up on the chair. He turned to his aunt, who put her finger to her lips and they tiptoed away.

'Your mum's fine,' she said. 'It can be one of your secrets, that dress. She likes to go dancing. She went last night, without your dad knowing. Your dad's a proud man but he's … strict. He wants to hold her close to him and he really doesn't understand how much she loves to dance.'

'So she keeps it quiet,' said Robbie.

Robbie felt such love for his mum. The flying pots, all the shouting, was because she felt trapped, like a bird in a cage. Perhaps this secret was a good secret, one that he could look at sometimes, like a treasure, and feel closer to her. She hadn't wanted Robbie to know, but he'd found out, and he felt glad. They had something in common. His dad kept them both under his thumb. He decided something. If his mum could have a secret life, so could he. And he wouldn't ever tell his dad her secret.

'Who does she go dancing with?' asked Robbie.

'Oh, just somebody … a nice young man,' said Aunt Mari. 'He's a great dancer, Rafferty. He used to be one of my pupils.'

Robbie and his mum walked back home together from Aunt Mari's house. Down on the port, the cranes were lifting huge containers, black against the bright sky. The cry of gulls and the smells of oil and seaweed were familiar. But there was another sensation awaiting him that wasn't familiar, and it wasn't pleasant either. There was a car with its engine idling, just in front of them.

Robbie felt his mum take his arm and they crossed the road.

'Pretend you haven't seen them, Robbie,' she said. The car drove ahead and then stopped again. Robbie made a mental note: a blue car, a Toyota, maybe a cab. He tried to memorise the number plate. They turned into Rappaport Road and walked towards their house.

'Let's walk on past our house,' said his mum. 'I don't want them to know where we live.'

Robbie remembered something. He said, 'Mum, I left my bike at Aunt Mari's.'

'We'll walk back there,' she said, speeding up her pace. She seemed really nervous, and this was when Robbie had the unfamiliar feeling. Apprehension.

They walked back down to the ferry port. Robbie saw, from the corner of his eye, a familiar figure. There he was: Jeff, on the docks, now wearing a work jacket and knitted hat. Was Jeff, workshy and shifty according to his dad, pretending to be one of the ferrymen? He seemed to be heading for the Cairnryan ferry. Robbie watched as he stepped on to the covered gangplank, slanting steeply up towards the deck. One more glimpse as he stepped on to the ship, and then Robbie lost sight of him.

Almost running now, Robbie's mum rushed up the steps of Aunt Mari's house and rang the bell. The car pulled up and a man in blue jeans got out. He was quite young, and pleased with himself it seemed to Robbie.

'Hey, Rose,' he said, 'are you trying to avoid me now?'

Robbie's mum smiled wanly.

'Hello, Rafferty,' she said.

'And who's this you've got with you?'

'He's my nephew, Robbie,' she said. Robbie glanced at his mum in shock. He felt his mother's hand descend quietly on his shoulder and give a sharp squeeze. Uncertain what to say, he opened his mouth and then shut it again. Who *was* this person?

'I wanted to see you again, Rose, but I didn't know where you lived,' said Rafferty.

Robbie looked at the stranger. He could feel the tension. Something was making his mother red in the face.

Rafferty ... *this* was the young man she went dancing with! He pretended to go and fetch his bike, which he'd left in the little alley running along the side of the house.

He was curious and, always ready to play the detective, he peered through the slats of the alley door. His mother was wrapping her coat tight around herself, in the same way Robbie did when he felt like he wanted to hide.

His aunt appeared at the door. 'Look what the cat brought in. Come in, Rafferty.'

'Hello, teacher,' said Rafferty, laughing.

The front door closed, but just as Robbie was about to get on his bike, he saw his dad's car driving up. His dad was here, and his mum's secret dancing friend was inside the house! He rushed up to the car, desperate to head him off.

'Dad!' he cried. 'Dad, I've just seen Jeff down by the ferry. He was dressed as a ferryman.' Robbie could see his dad was not in a good mood.

'What's it to you?' he said angrily. But, after a moment, he turned and got back in the car, muttering, 'That's it. Do someone a good turn. Why did I bother?'

'What is it, Dad?' said Robbie.

'I found Jeff a good job at the port,' growled his dad. 'Not on the boats. He's not fit for that – or anything else, it seems.'

And he drove off, tyres screeching, as Robbie breathed a sigh of relief.

Aunt Lizzie had come over to get news of Jeff. Robbie was wondering if he ought to mention the fact that his cousin had actually boarded the ferry, but he didn't want Jeff to get into trouble. He decided to keep quiet.

He pretended to do his maths homework on the kitchen table, but really he was listening. A detective needed to find out what was going on. It might be important.

'Are you working the boy too hard on his first day?' Aunt Lizzie said to his dad. 'Jeff hasn't come home yet and he's not answering his phone.'

'No, the little blighter skived off this morning – on his first day, mind. He was spotted near the Cairnryan ferry. Since then no one has seen him at all.'

'Are you serious?' Aunt Lizzie sounded upset.

'I am,' said Mark, 'but why don't you ring Mari? Robbie often goes there after school and I expect Jeff drops in there too. He must be somewhere, but that's the end of a job on the docks for him. I reckon you went and got yourself nothing but trouble when you adopted that one.'

Robbie's mum came into the room with some glasses and a bottle of orange liqueur left over from Christmas. She poured her sister a drink. His dad looked disapprovingly at her and left the room.

'Oh, Rose, I'm dead worried about Jeff,' said Lizzie. 'I have a feeling something's wrong. I wish I'd never let him leave school, but the boy was doing no good there and you know what – he hated it.'

Robbie glanced up from his homework and could see Aunt Lizzie was almost weeping. His mum patted her hand.

'The only thing he enjoyed was the rowing club. He was in the school crew, he did so well – he loves the sea. He was never happier than when he was in a boat. But since he left school he just mooches around. There's not much for lads to do round here, I suppose.'

Now Robbie could hear she was crying.

'Well, it seems Robbie saw Jeff down by the ferry this morning,' said Rose, 'and that was the last anyone saw of him. Will you go to the police about Jeff?'

'God, no!' said Aunt Lizzie. 'I'm afraid Jeff may be up to his neck in something.'

CHAPTER 3

The wasps' nest

Rose and Robbie had a close bond, as if they were joined by a web of fine underground threads, mysteriously in touch at a deeper level.

Robbie knew his mum had never been one for domestic life; she wasn't remotely interested in making things cosy. Robbie remembered her holding up a soggy dishcloth and saying, 'This thing makes me want to scream!' as she threw it hard at the fridge.

Meals were minimal. A cheese-and-ham toastie was about the most complex thing on the table many days. Robbie usually ate fast and disappeared upstairs.

He was back at school after the holidays and today everything had been so awful. After supper he went to his room. As he sat by the window, looking out, he saw a drowsy winter wasp on the windowsill and remembered watching the wasps come and go from the eaves of the house last summer. The papery nest was over his bedroom window and at night, when the wind was still and heat hung in the air, Robbie could hear the soft sounds of the wasps, as if the entire nest was gently humming, louder and softer, louder and softer, as the whole swarm fanned their wings to a breathing rhythm, keeping the nest cool.

Wasps are neither malignant or kind – they're only being

themselves – but a swarm can do a lot of damage with its venomous stings when it's roused.

The wasps reminded Robbie of the boys in his class. Today, at lunch break, everyone seemed to be looking at him, sharing a joke and exchanging glances as he sat alone with his lunch. He heard his name from all directions, and he heard noisy gossip about Jeff disappearing. Robbie's cousin was a loser, he was on the run… Robbie felt the sting of their comments. An awful boy called Dodds was leading the swarm, nudging his fellows and making sure that Robbie heard it all.

Robbie had come home after the last class with a miserable expression and slumped shoulders.

'What's happened?' asked his mum.

'Nothing,' said Robbie. He needed a bit of time before he could talk about it. The gossip had got him down. And then there were the noises…

After lunch, when Robbie had begun to answer a question in history, everyone started coughing, scraping their chairs back, shuffling their feet, and tapping pencils on the desktops. Robbie's voice was drowned out. He stopped. He felt suffocated.

Mr Burton told them off, and that made matters worse.

'That's enough! Quiet there. You would do better to listen to what Robbie has to say – he's brighter than the rest of you put together and you can all learn something.'

They stopped their noises, but at the end of the lesson two of the boys, Dodds and Victor, had hustled up to him, poking him and nudging him.

'You're the clever one, aren't you?'

'But your Jeff's a runaway.'

'What's your cousin up to?'

'He's done a runner. Your family – in trouble, is it?'

Robbie got away but his heart was pounding.

After a while, Robbie decided to go and sit with his mum. She put her arm round his shoulders and he told her everything. She looked upset. She gave him a hug and put on the television. They sat together companionably for half an hour.

After tea, although it was cold and dark, he decided to go out on his bike. He pedalled down to the port.

I don't want to go back to school. If I say anything they'll drown me out with their noises. They think I'm showing off. I'm only trying to stay out of trouble. Still, it's good that I've got something interesting in my casebook.

I'm going to see if I can find Jeff. I'm a witness now, as well as a detective. I spotted him down at the docks. Dad and Aunt Mari asked me lots of questions but I didn't mention the man he met there. I wanted to remember it exactly right and thought that if I'd written it down, it would be easy. But it's hard to write when you're using binoculars. I don't know how anyone does it. And wouldn't it make people look at me? Which is not a good thing for a detective.

Anyway, if I'd been writing I'd have missed seeing Jeff. He looked kind of jumpy. He looked nervous. If I keep looking for him, he's bound to turn up eventually. And I'm going to look for that short man he got the package from. I know what he looks like. If I see him, I'll follow him and find out who he is.

A week later, Robbie was still watching the port regularly to see who was around. He'd been to visit Aunt Mari with his mum and he pretended not to be interested in what they were saying. He heard that Aunt Lizzie was very afraid for Jeff and maybe knew something about his whereabouts, but she didn't want to say anything. Nobody, in any case, had any time for the police in Arlen.

CHAPTER 4

Those in peril on the sea

Robbie stood on the cliff by the Princess Victoria Memorial with his dad, waiting for the band to start up. There was a crowd waiting for the wreath-laying ceremony to remember those who had lost their lives at sea. His dad had told him the story.

On this day in January 1953, the *Princess Victoria* ferry set out from Stranraer in Scotland, heading for the port of Arlen. There was foul weather and a bad forecast, but it was a short journey.

When the ferry headed out of the lough into the sea, with Arlen almost 20 miles away, the huge steel doors to the car deck, which also served as the ramp, were still open.

The captain, unaware, was heading into an epic storm that lashed the whole of the British Isles on that day and brought havoc and destruction, drowning sheep, cattle, horses and people. Piers, jetties and seaside bungalows were tossed in the air and left, upended, half buried in sand.

Robbie listened as his dad told him how waves began slopping into the car deck at the open hatch. The crew tried desperately to raise the ramp, but the mechanism jammed. Soon huge waves were crashing into the car deck. In the teeth of the storm, unable to turn round, the ship battled on. The *Princess Victoria* needed a tug boat to get her back to Stranraer.

His dad said that by then many other boats were in trouble and sending out SOS messages; all the tugs and lifeboats were busy and help could not come.

A fast lifeboat finally set out from Scotland to look for the ferry, but the rescuers couldn't find the *Princess Victoria*.

Robbie started to worry that this story wasn't going to end well.

His dad had gone on to describe how, as the stricken ship began to keel over, her lifeboats were made ready. Women and children, clutching at each other, piled into the small wooden boats and dropped down into the icy cauldron of waves. The rescue boat found them at last and was joined by others.

Robbie sighed with relief. Help was at hand.

But the rescue ships were held back by the gale and the giant waves, and couldn't get close enough to the sinking ship, so the little boats were pulled down with the ship as it sank. Of the 176 people on board, only 42 were rescued. None of the crew left their posts and none survived.

His dad said he'd wanted Robbie to understand why the crew were still honoured for their bravery.

Robbie more than understood. He felt devastated.

Today, out on the promontory, by the sturdy stone column of the Chaine Memorial Tower, a solemn crowd had turned up. The sun was coming out after days of stormy skies. Many people there were connected with ships or the port, and some had lost husbands, fathers, or sons to the sea.

From his vantage point beside his dad, Robbie watched a procession of beefy lifeboat men, who were followed by white-faced men in suits and red-faced men in kilts. Then came several women in expensive-looking coats; they took their turn laying wreaths on the memorial. A keen wind blew in from the North Channel, ruffling the kilts of the band. There were bagpipes behind the pipers and, lastly, the deep boom of the enormous Lambeg drum, known as a big slapper and the loudest drum in the world. The heart-rending skirl of the bagpipes prompted tears of collective grief. Everyone sang, 'Oh hear us when we cry to thee, for those in peril on the sea'.

So many of those in peril had drowned, Robbie found it hard to believe the Lord was listening.

He had to find a way out of this deep pool of sorrow. He wiped his face on his sleeve and took out his binoculars. He'd decided that the way forward in his investigations was to see things and write them down when he got home.

He moved his binoculars across the faces. Now, in the extraordinary way that adults have when at a solemn event, a funeral for example, the crowd threw off the burden of their grief; all the mourners started chattering like starlings and laughing with the joy of being alive after the sorrowful moments of the wreath-laying. Several of the men were wearing sunglasses and now looked as if they were on holiday and hadn't a care in the world.

There was someone Robbie recognised. He couldn't place him...

'Dad.' He nudged his father. 'Who's that man over there?'

'What man?'

'The man wearing the baggy old coat,' he said, pointing.

'Don't point, it's rude, and that's a duffel coat,' said his dad, looking grim. 'I wouldn't have anything at all to do with a man like that. I hear he's a bookie or something on the Isle of Man. They're all money-laundering crooks. He sometimes stays in a flat in one of the houses near to ours. He uses the ferry a lot.'

'What's money-laundering mean?' whispered Robbie.

'People bring him their dirty money and he washes it for them, son,' said his dad, with a tight smile.

Robbie wasn't at all sure if his father was joking, so he kept quiet and looked hard at the man. All at once, he knew who it was, and his stomach turned cold. That was Aunt Mari's boyfriend.

Robbie was freezing when he got home. His teeth were chattering. His favourite fleece hadn't been able to stand up to the sadness of the occasion, the deep throb of the drums, the standing about while his dad chatted to the influential men of his lodge, and the shivery feeling of seeing Aunt Mari's boyfriend.

His mum ran him a bath and left a big soft towel on the sink. He jumped in, the water stinging at first with the contrast.

They'd all been even more silent than usual around the house. He rather wanted to have a conversation. If they could talk more it would help. He could hear his mum moving around on the landing, just outside the door.

He picked up the sponge, which had been floating on the water, considering it. He shouted to his mum, 'Maybe if a boat was made like a sponge, with lots of little air holes in, it wouldn't sink.'

She didn't seem to find this an interesting thought, so he tried another tack.

'Do you think Aunt Mari has a boyfriend?'

That got her attention. He heard her stop moving.

'What makes you say that?' she said sharply.

'Oh, I don't know,' he said, pretending not to be very interested in the reply. This was hard. 'She's so nice, and her house is big.'

'Well, we'll just have to wait until she finds the right one, Robbie. There are plenty of wrong ones around!'

'Has she got a wrong one then?'

'No, of course not, I was only saying,' she said.

His mum was a bad liar. He could hear it in the tone of her voice. Hiding something, he thought. For Robbie, catching his mum in another lie was a moment of truth. We all have our secrets, he thought. What were the words of that song they were learning to sing in the choir at school?

'We can never see the heart.'

His mum was covering up for Aunt Mari, and he was covering up for both his aunt and his mum. But was he protecting Jeff as well? He'd never been sure about Jeff. But perhaps Jeff needed help. Maybe he'd done something wrong and had to leave and Robbie didn't want to make life harder for him. What had Jeff done, though? He needed to find out.

And who *was* Aunt Mari's boyfriend? He was mysterious and his mum didn't want to talk about him. That wasn't a good sign.

CHAPTER 5

Following

It was the weekend and Robbie was down at the docks again. In the holidays he'd been able to come most mornings on his bike. Then term had started and he could only come after school or at weekends.

It was cold, grey, and a bit misty, and he didn't think he would want to stay long. He was taking a quick look through his binoculars at the passengers coming off the Cairnryan ferry. He was looking for Jeff and the small man in the leather jacket. Could he be the one? It looked like him. At last! Robbie prepared to follow him.

The man looked well dressed. He had on a tight sheepskin bomber jacket. He had a sort of neat cleanliness shining from him, unlike most of the dishevelled people getting off the ferry. He walked lightly from the port and found a taxi. Robbie got on his bike and started to follow.

The taxi set off and Robbie was able to keep it in sight as it crawled, in heavy traffic, through the town and on to Bridge Street, then up the hill. It stopped outside the old library, no longer only a library but now the repository of everything to do with Arlen's industrial past and its maritime history and famous ships. It had special rooms for performing live music and for local groups to meet up. It was called the Arlen

Museum, Library and Arts Centre, but most people just called it the arts centre. Who'd have thought a town once known as the toilet of Northern Ireland would have its very own arts centre?

It worked out well, because Robbie could park his bike and go inside. And *there* was the man! He had a little bag with him, Robbie noticed, which he put on the counter when he started talking to the receptionist.

'It's Windy Wake for Rory O'Connor.'

The receptionist's hair was dyed a sugary pink and she was dressed in white dungarees, her face as pale and round and powdery as a cream puff. She looked at the man as if she wanted to throw herself on him and give him a kiss.

'Lovely to see you again, Mr Wake!' she said.

'An appointment,' he said. 'For ten o'clock. With the director.'

He stood looking around and smiled at Robbie, who smiled back and then pretended to look at the pamphlets on the desk.

'Welcome to Arlen Arts Centre, Mr Wake. Mr O'Connor will be down in a minute. Won't you please take a chair?'

The small man removed his sheepskin jacket and sat down to wait.

Robbie went over to an exhibit board and started to read up on the filming of *Game of Thrones*. Some scenes had been shot in Magheramorne Quarry, which wasn't far from Arlen. Then there were the Dark Hedges. Maybe he could persuade his mum to take him one day.

A sleek, dark-haired man, rubbing his hands and looking welcoming, came down the stairs, glided across the parquet floor and took Windy Wake's hand in both of his.

'It's such a real pleasure and an honour to have you here,' he said. 'Let's go up to my office.'

So now Robbie knew Jeff's mysterious friend was called Windy Wake. He'd been friendly and he seemed to Robbie like a very old child, he was so small.

He looked at the girl with pink hair, who was using a tiny brush to colour her nails black. He wanted to know what Windy Wake was doing here.

'I saw that visitor down by the ferry,' he said chattily.

'Oh, did you now?' The girl gave him a quick once over. 'And what makes you so interested in him?' she asked.

Robbie was rather taken aback – she was sharper than he thought she'd be.

'Oh, well, I just wondered, you know,' he said, rather feebly. He didn't mention Jeff.

'Well, he's a dancer, quite famous, and he's going to help my boss put on a show here. He'll be the choreographer and musical director, if you want to know.'

'What's a choreographer?' said Robbie. The girl smiled at him.

'He shows the dancers how to do their dance. There'll be singing as well,' said the girl, flapping her hands from the wrists and blowing on her fingernails. 'We're doing a musical called *Little Shop of Horrors*.'

'Can I come to it?' he said.

'Sure you can. It's not till Valentine's Day. The cast will be rehearsing in the Carrick Hall for two weeks before that if you want to see them. I'll be there myself. The first time we all meet up is Saturday, but after that it will be mainly weekdays. All the performers will be local and we'll be rehearsing a lot. It's quite hard, every evening for two weeks. There'll be children in it, so it has to be later, as everyone's at school all day or have their jobs, you see. I'm Julie, by the way. Who are you?'

'I'm Robbie.'

'Well, Robbie, you can sign my visitors' book,' she said, 'since you're the only visitor I've had today, apart from Windy Wake.'

She came out from behind the desk with the book and a pen, holding them gingerly to avoid smudging her black nails.

'OK, Robbie,' she said. 'I'll see you for the casting of the musical at six thirty at the Carrick Hall next Saturday.' She gave him a coloured leaflet about the musical. 'Don't forget, now! And don't worry, I'll see that you get along just fine.'

I'm very excited because we're going to the Carrick Hall tonight. Today is the day of the first meeting for the musical that Julie told me about. Mum made some sort of special eggs for breakfast. They were supposed to be scrambled – but they looked as if she'd dropped them on the floor and scraped them up. She wanted to please Dad – it seemed to work as she persuaded him to let us go to it. I'd shown her the leaflet and she got quite excited. She loves music, but Dad is so strict. If she starts to play her favourite songs he says, 'Turn that unholy racket off!' And they hardly ever go out anywhere, except to chapel.

The musical is called *Little Shop of Horrors* but Mum didn't mention the name. She just said it's for children. And Dad said, 'As long as there are no dodgy people there. If there are, bring Robbie straight home.'

I hope I won't bump into those boys from school. I think they're dead dodgy.

Robbie and his mum, bundled up against the cold, walked through an insistent whirl of snow to the Carrick Hall. Each street light had a golden halo of flakes falling softly through the glow and vanishing into the dark. Robbie watched the car drivers leaning forwards like jockeys heading for the finishing post and hooting at those in front; everyone in a hurry to get home before the snow settled too deeply or froze to ice.

Once inside the hall they plunged into a warm wash of steaming bodies swathed in fleeces and puffas, with shoes and boots dripping and faces radiating with the pleasure of having arrived.

Shouts of 'We got here!' and 'You made it!' echoed round the hall as people shook coats and umbrellas and dumped them on the tables lining the walls. Many boys and girls were removing their outdoor boots and getting what looked like gym shoes and ballet shoes out of cotton bags.

Robbie had never been to the hall before. Unlike the friendly arts centre – a place of quiet calm, scented with the wafting particles of dry, dusty pages – this place was huge and greeted the visitor with a noticeably human smell. Inside the hall the walls were lined with wood. There were rows of folding chairs, painted a vivid green, set out where the dance floor had been. A raised platform remained dark and mysterious at the far end. Robbie breathed in air that was thick with a mixture of excitement and anxiety. Friends were greeting each other, seeming relieved at seeing someone familiar. There was a general buzz of excitement.

Robbie got rid of his coat and started looking around. He saw one or two boys from his school, but they were older. And then he saw Julie in the crowd, her pink hair shining like candy floss. She was wearing her white dungarees and, on her bare arms, long, black, lace, fingerless gloves.

He wondered if she would remember him and he waved tentatively. When she saw Robbie she made her way towards him, and her face lit up. 'I wondered if you'd come,' she said.

He felt glad to see her. 'This is my mum, Rose. Mum, this is Julie.'

Rose's eyebrows were raised, and Robbie thought maybe she was surprised that he had an older friend with pink hair. They all went to find seats near the front which, by now, was just about impossible.

They searched for a space among couples in sports clothes and large men with shaved heads and tattooed necks. There were groomed men with beards dressed in neat tweeds, mothers with girls dressed up in fairy outfits, and teenagers wearing T-shirts proclaiming *Stop Fracking* and *I'd Rather be Sleeping*.

They found somewhere and Robbie's mum started

gossiping with a friend she'd seen. Robbie sat between his mother and Julie. He overheard the friend asking about Jeff.

'Jeff's still missing,' said his mum, 'but Lizzie heard he's been seen in Port Glasgow and she told me he's looking different.'

'What, in disguise, do you mean?'

'Well, not in disguise exactly. No, what's strange is that he looks better, nicer clothes.'

Then they started talking about Aunt Mari and her boyfriend. His mum was whispering, and as Robbie strained to hear he thought he caught the word 'investigator', but Julie interrupted.

'Do you know what an audition is?'

'I think so,' said Robbie, detaching himself from his eavesdropping.

'It's when they try to find singers and dancers for the show. They want local people to be part of it.'

'I can sing,' said Robbie. 'I'm in the school choir. We sing hymns and Irish folk songs and stuff like that.'

'Well then,' said Julie, 'you're in with a chance.'

'My mum can sing really well too. My grandad was a musician. She has a lot of songs she likes to sing, she's really good. But she hasn't been singing much lately.'

Julie leaned over towards Rose. 'Robbie tells me you've a great voice,' she said. 'You should have a go at auditioning for the chorus.'

There was a sudden hush as the hall darkened and the stage glowed with golden spotlights. On to the stage stepped a tall woman in fringed leather trousers and an embroidered suede waistcoat, who looked, at first glance, like a young ranch hand.

'Hey there, y'all!' she said, smiling and nodding her head. She waved her arms in welcome, turquoise and silver bracelets jangling. Robbie liked her immediately. She seemed to glow as she stood in the spotlight with her long silvery-grey hair.

'Hey, my singers of songs, welcome! Isn't it just wonderful to see so many of you on a snowy night like this – we don't get too many of them in Kentucky! I expect y'all thought you were auditioning for *The Snowman*.'

The audience laughed. She went on. 'I'm Susie Paltrow, they call me SP, yes sir. I'm a country and western singer right to the heart. I sing about love and I play guitar. I'm the one who'll be looking out for talent tonight, together with my good friend, the fabulous dancer and choreographer, Windy Wake!'

At this point a neat little figure stepped on to the stage. He bowed. Robbie's skin prickled as he saw the man he'd been following, the one Julie had admired at the arts centre, the one who knew Jeff.

SP introduced him. 'We're so lucky to have him here with us, auditioning and helping to put this musical together. OK, campers, let's all welcome Wind-ee Wake.'

She started clapping, and everyone in the audience cheered and clapped as he came on stage, even though Robbie suspected they'd only a vague idea who Windy Wake was.

Next, Robbie recognised Julie's boss from the arts centre, groomed and smartly dressed, as he walked lightly on to the stage and introduced himself with a charming smile.

'Hello, everyone! Nice to see such a big turnout on such a wintry night. Getting together to put on this show will, we hope, offer our community a wonderful sense of common purpose...' Robbie, along with most of the audience, started to shuffle his feet. O'Connor's little speech fell on deaf ears. A buzz of conversation started up. After only a couple more minutes he gave up, and introduced Miss Shirley, the pianist, a serious-looking girl in her early twenties, who bowed to the audience, said 'Hi everyone!' and took over the piano.

SP came back on to the stage and instantly filled it with the joy and exuberance of her presence.

'Let's audition for the junior choir. Please will all you lovelies of ten or under who want to sing come up here with me. Don't be shy, now.'

There were a couple of high-pitched cries of 'I don't want to', and even a sob or two, but a brave band of young children bounded up to the stage and mounted the steps at the side, encouraged by Miss Shirley. She took them into a little room to the side of the stage.

Robbie looked at Julie. She whispered in his ear. 'How old are you?'

'I'm nearly fifteen,' he lied, hoping a couple of years wouldn't matter between friends.

There was a lull, with an increasing hum of chat from the audience, and then the small children emerged. They varied in size and some could sing – although some decidedly couldn't, and were returned with comforting noises to their disappointed parents. Miss Shirley ended up with six promising young singers.

Now it was the eleven-to-sixteens. His mum leaned over. 'Will you have a go, Robbie? I think you'd like it.'

'I will if you will, Mum.'

'*Can* I take part in it?' she said, caught off guard.

'Yes, you can, and I'll do it if you will too – so it's not just me, but both of us and we can persuade Dad.'

Julie bent over towards Robbie's mum and whispered, 'So, Rose, what have you got to lose?'

Robbie looked at her hopefully.

'Well ... go on then,' she said to Robbie. 'If you get picked I'll have a go. I suppose there's no harm in trying!'

His heart bounding in his chest, Robbie went forward and up on to the stage. A disparate bunch of adolescents stood in a huddle, wondering what to do next. They didn't look very much like starlets in waiting, except for one: a tall girl with very long, shiny hair, whose expression seemed to Robbie to have been put on with her outfit – a sparkly silver top and leggings. Robbie, always the detective, watched and waited.

'Step forward if you can sing,' said Windy Wake. They all stepped forward.

'Now, I want you all to listen carefully to this,' said Miss Shirley, 'and then we'll all sing it together.'

She struck up 'My Bonnie Lies Over the Ocean'.

All the children took a deep breath and their voices rang out.

'That was a pipe opener for you,' said Miss Shirley. 'We always need to do a warm-up first to get our voices clear.'

They were given a sheet of paper with the words and music of 'Amazing Grace'.

The confident, sparkly girl, who introduced herself as Maddy, went first. The happy buzz of gossip in the hall was getting louder.

'Now I want you folks to listen,' said SP. 'Let's give these children a chance.'

The buzz died out, with shushes from here and there. Robbie waited breathlessly.

Miss Shirley started to play. Maddy sang the gospel song with a pure and tuneful voice. Robbie looked at his mum in the audience. Her face was neutral. He knew what she'd be thinking – that this girl had a lovely voice but there was no real *feeling*. She'd always told Robbie how important that was. Robbie knew she'd be willing him to put more into it.

Three more children sang the song unexceptionally. Now it was his turn.

He'd heard the way his mother sang, swaying with the music and putting her soul into it. He was nervous and a little shaky, but he tried to do it the way she would like it. Robbie had really listened to the words sung by those four singers, and found 'Amazing Grace' to be a very emotional song; the singer is thanking God for saving him. He was actually blind, but now, thanks to the grace of God, he can see. A miracle! Even his dad would approve.

Robbie's pure, light voice was soaring, drawing each person there into the heartbreaking feeling of the song.

When he finished there was a roar of approval and he looked over towards his mum. She and Julie were clapping; just about everyone was applauding, even the other child singers were whooping and encouraging him.

The adults finally went up to sing. Robbie, tingling with pleasure, sat with Julie, who said she could dance but couldn't sing to save her granny.

Robbie could see his mum was nervous; her shoulders were up and she was breathing too fast. Miss Shirley started to play. He saw his mum straighten up as she began to sing. She was singing one of her own favourites, a song from *West Side Story* called 'There's a Place For Us'. Her fine voice gathered strength and the blue notes of a warm summer dusk filled the hall.

There was a loud thump as the heavy hall doors were hurled open, and sounds of a commotion followed. Robbie turned round to see his dad thundering towards the stage like a charging bull, his face suffused with an ugly purple. Hurrying after him was Aunt Lizzie's husband, Uncle Martin, trying to grab him from behind. Robbie turned back to see his mum frozen on the stage. He felt sick.

'I know all about you, Rory O'Connor,' bellowed his dad. 'Where are you? What do you mean by teaching my son this filth?' He shook the brochure for the show in the air.

Rory O'Connor, director of the arts centre, stepped on to the stage and looked calmly at Robbie's dad.

'Is there a problem here?' he said. 'Have you got something

you'd like to discuss later? We're in the middle of auditions at the moment, so please have the courtesy to sit down until we finish.' His voice was firm and filled with disdain.

'Would you look at that?' shouted Robbie's dad, now brought to a standstill in his charge towards the stage. Robbie followed his gaze and saw his mum, magnificent in the green velvet dress she'd borrowed from Aunt Mari, standing firmly on the stage, facing the audience with a look of defiance on her face.

'That's my wife up there with that abomination, that fiend in disguise, that ungodly man!' he shouted.

Now some members of the audience were on their feet shouting 'Sit down!' Some were laughing. There was a flash and then another. Someone was taking photographs.

Through the mayhem Rory O'Connor shouted, 'This is a public gathering, where people are free to express their views at the right time. But this is way beyond what we accept. I believe the mayor, Mr McCleod, is here. Could you please ask this gentleman to leave?'

Mayor Dev McCleod was there, perspiring in the front row from what Robbie could see. He stood up and shot a look of dislike at Rory O'Connor. Perhaps he hadn't wanted to get involved.

'Will everyone sit down!' he bellowed. 'And Mr Laggan! What is this? This is intolerable, you are causing a disturbance. Kindly do not open your mouth again, or I will call the police.'

I'm worried about my dad. He's losing it in front of

everyone and they're laughing at him and he's spoiling everything. What was he on about, teaching me filth? No one here seems to be frightened of him; they don't like him, they all shouted at him to sit down and he has. But I bet he's going to be angry when we get home. I hope Mum gets another chance to sing. He interrupted her song.

Windy Wake is talking to my dad, he's asking him to leave. Dad's getting up and Uncle Martin is going too. Dad asks me to go with him, but I really want to stay. Mum is staying, she's talking to SP, but I'll have to go home with him. I'd better get my coat.

Now it's just me and Dad. I've never seen him so ballistic. He's all purple in the face and shouting about a place in hell for all the people in the hall. He went and scraped the car on a bollard, which made him even worse.

He's furious with Mum and he told me he was saving me from all sorts of profanity. I don't know that word, I'll have to look it up .

Aunt Mari came over to get Mum's things and she told him not to expect Mum home tonight and that she's going to stay with her. Dad didn't like that one bit. Mum sent me a message that she'll be back tomorrow morning to sort things out. It's times like this I wish Dad would let us have mobile phones. Then Mum could send me messages herself without needing Aunt Mari to pass them on.

Dad made me a sandwich and sent me upstairs to bed. But I want to keep an eye on him. I can see him, just his shoulders and the top of his head, if I sit on the stairs. He's sitting there, rocking backwards and forwards, reading his Bible and muttering to himself.

I hope he's going to calm down soon.

It doesn't look as if he's going to go to bed, though.

I'm going to bed. I'll see Mum tomorrow.

In the twilight you never really see the moment the tide turns in the lough, when the steely swell, with ripples like tarnished old silver, more black than grey, suddenly decides to change direction and smoothly, silkily, starts to flood out of the harbour mouth, dragging everything along with it, out to sea.

CHAPTER 6

The lobster

It's Sunday and I'm alone in the house with Dad. I don't like it when Mum's away. He's very quiet this morning. He says we're going to chapel.

He thinks I'm spoiled. I'm not living in the spirit of what the Lord wants. He told me in the car on the way home last night that Mum has given me too much rope. I think that means that he expects I'll hang myself with it. I've heard that before.

I hope I do get chosen for the chorus and then I'll show him what I can do. I wonder how I'll get to the rehearsals... I hope Mum will come and get me.

I'm going to ask her if I can get Little Shop of Horrors on DVD if she comes back – I might be able to watch it while Dad's still at the docks if I get home from school quickly. But I'll have to hide it. He won't want me watching it. He thinks it's called *The Rocky Horror Show*, which is wrong. I told him.

And I still want to hunt for Jeff and find out what's happened to him.

Before dragging him off to chapel, Robbie's dad gave him a severe telling off. He told Robbie the musical was going to twist his mind, and that Rory O'Connor was trying to harm him in some way. Robbie was mystified, but could tell how convinced his dad was by the look on his face – laced with veins, eyes bulging – just like a preacher in a pulpit who works himself up into a frenzy in his efforts to convince the congregation that they will be punished if they don't believe him. After chapel he'd calmed down and settled in the kitchen with his local newspaper, the *Arlen Post*, as usual. Robbie walked past, but stopped when the front page caught his eye. There, right in the centre, was a picture of his dad with eyes glaring, mouth agape as he shouted in the Carrick Hall, under the headline FERRY MASTER CAUSES AUDITION RUMPUS.

Underneath was a smaller picture of Robbie's mum standing on the stage, looking tragic. His dad threw the paper down and left the room. Robbie picked it up and read.

> Our ferry master, a pillar of his local Orange Lodge and a well-known figure of the town, caused a scene at the auditions in the Carrick Hall last night. He was verbally chastised by the mayor and escorted from the hall by dance celebrity Windy Wake. Mark Laggan, 45, removed his young son Robbie, aged 13, a promising singer who'd auditioned earlier, declaring that he did not want him performing in *Little Shop of Horrors*.

Robbie's dad shut himself up in the sitting room and Robbie didn't dare go near him. Nor did he want to.

He went and got his bike.

An hour later Robbie appeared at Aunt Mari's house, holding a plastic bag. He'd come by the harbour. The snow was mostly melted, the tide was high and the brownish water looked oily. Some battered fishing boats were tied up and a group of young fishermen in woolly hats, their cheeks red with the cold, were having a chat on the quay as they sorted out their nets and lobster and crab pots.

No fishing boats had been out because of the weather, so when Robbie went to say hello to them, they had nothing to show him but a blue and black lobster that one of them, Sandy, had kept overnight in a bucket of seawater.

'Here you are,' said Sandy, 'give it to your ma and ask her to cook it for you. I saw her picture in the paper today – I wish her well.' Robbie thanked him. He was happy with the gift; he'd never had a lobster before.

But his aunt didn't have a big enough pot for the poor thing. Neither she nor his mum had much of an idea how to cook such an alarming-looking creature. So they took it round to Aunt Lizzie and Uncle Martin's house.

Uncle Martin was in a state, trying to explain to them that Robbie's dad had come round last night in a great rage. He'd wanted to stop him from going to the hall, but he hadn't had a hope. Robbie's mum tried to reassure him.

'I know it, it's awful, he gets so het up. Honestly, nothing can stop him once he starts a rant.'

They found a large pot and when it was boiling Uncle Martin steamed the lobster. It went brick red. They let it cool down and then the five of them sat down to lunch and Robbie decided he quite liked lobster with melted butter.

Robbie looked forward to seeing Julie whenever he could get to the arts centre. He was glad to find someone who was so interested in people watching, someone he could talk to and find she thought the same as him.

Julie overflowed with curiosity about everything. She brought colour and a bit of fun into Robbie's life, which he badly needed. She took him under her wing and enjoyed telling him things. His eagerness to find out everything made him a very good audience.

Tonight was the dance audition and Julie would be there. The gossipmongers, after reading about the first audition in the local newspaper, had decided to go and see for themselves and the hall was busy. The night was frosty and, once again, everybody was bundled up in their puffas and fleeces. It was like Christmas, with people laughing and chatting as they made their way to the Carrick Hall. By the time everybody had piled in, the hall was jammed.

Robbie tracked down Julie, who was noticeable in the crush with her leopard-print catsuit and her pink hair twisted in a frizzy topknot. She'd saved seats for Robbie and his mum. His two aunts had come along too, and managed to squeeze in alongside.

To Robbie's relief, his mum had come back home at teatime. Apparently, Aunt Mari had told her she would be an idiot if she didn't.

'You'll lose all your rights,' she'd said. 'You and I both know what happens – like Rosaleen Blackwood. She lives with her mam now and she hardly gets to see her children.' His mum told him she hadn't wanted to risk that.

Windy Wake came to the front of the stage. He held up his hand for silence.

'Hello everyone! For those who weren't at the last audition, I'm Windy Wake. You can call me Windy. I want you all to know, darlings, dancing is the biggest buzz ever, so let yourself go.'

'I wonder why he wanted to come to Arlen,' whispered his mum to Aunt Mari.

'I wonder why *anyone* wants to come to Arlen,' said Aunt Mari, laughing.

The auditions began. The little children put on their performances one by one. Some forgot the steps and one dinky dancer froze to the spot sucking her fingers. Some got overexcited and showed off so much they fell over. Some tried to do rapping, one or two looked warlike, kicking and stamping, and out of the motley crew Windy picked the few who could move in time to the music.

'OK, now,' said Windy, beckoning the next group of waiting dancers. 'Come on, people, only one thing to do – give your all, darlings, give me everything you've got.'

Robbie's mum got up. Robbie sat in the audience with his two aunts. He hoped his mum wouldn't be embarrassing. Singing was OK, but dancing? He was willing her to change her mind about it. He was also puzzling about the famous dancer.

Windy Wake is on the stage. I don't get it. They say he's a celebrity. What was he doing with Jeff, handing him a package? Maybe Julie knows something.

I think there's something fishy going on. Jeff might be a smuggler, but it has to be something small. I expect there were diamonds in the envelope. Maybe Jeff has run off with them, and the people who were expecting to get the priceless jewels are tracking him down, so he's had to hide. But what about Windy? Is he a diamond smuggler too?

With the staccato beat of a drum as well as the piano, the music was energising and it was very clear that Robbie's mum could really dance. Windy applauded each dancer and he clapped Julie too. He whooped enthusiastically when she managed to fit in a couple of cartwheels, as a bonus, as she danced.

Robbie was thrilled when his mum and Julie were chosen to perform along with six other dancers. He was now all set to spend most of the next two weeks with his mum at the hall; she would be either watching Robbie or rehearsing herself. His dad would not be happy.

When Robbie asked Julie about Windy Wake she seemed to know a great deal. He'd started as a classically trained ballet dancer. As a boy he was so light on his feet he could fly through the air like a grasshopper. But he was nicknamed Widget by the members of his London ballet school because he didn't grow. The leading parts he hoped for always went to taller boys. In low spirits, he abandoned his training and went to Toronto, where he found his niche in contemporary dance.

Julie had heard that he fell on his feet, made friends and ended up dancing with small, experimental dance companies.

Nothing Robbie heard came anywhere near explaining how Windy and Jeff knew each other.

CHAPTER 7

A hard man

Robbie went back to the woods. It was quite early on Sunday afternoon. The sun was low and the bluish light was good; he'd discovered that binoculars work much better on a bright day. He'd done the lunch dishes and tried, with his mum, to persuade his dad about the singing – she didn't mention the dancing.

He'd left them arguing.

According to what Robbie had read, the whole town disapproved of his dad's bursting into the hall. Probably his dad was beginning to understand that he'd got it all wrong, making such a scene in front of the mayor.

Robbie's dad had been brought up in Arlen in a very strict household. He'd told Robbie that his grandfather's creed was, 'Obey God, obey the word of the Bible, and obey your father who knows what's right for you. Disobey, and the Lord will punish you. Do as I say, or you will be chastised. Spare the rod and spoil the child.'

And being a boy, and a stubborn-minded boy at that, Robbie's dad was chastised often in the name of the Lord. He'd had to learn to stifle his feelings.

Robbie had never been beaten by his dad. His discipline was confined to hectoring, virtually thumping him over the head with Bible talk and red-raw shouting.

Robbie had always thought of his dad as solid, a pillar of great strength. But there were cracks appearing. Nobody in the hall had come to his side. Now his dad, used to being respected, was a figure of fun and, like a wounded animal, was hiding away and snarling at anyone who came near – including Robbie.

But Robbie had learned how to switch off and how to disappear. He went to his hideaway under the oak tree. He'd brought with him a couple of cold potatoes hidden in his pocket from lunch, to keep him going in the cold. He was wearing gloves and this made it hard to adjust the binoculars.

He reckoned that now Jeff had disappeared, he was safe to go back to his old vantage point opposite the back of his house. He tucked himself into his usual place and looked at the kitchen. Nothing much happening. His mum seemed to have gone out. He was noticing things about the houses on the steep hillside facing him: the usual fishing nets hanging out on a balcony; black, spiky frosted flowers in a trough on another; and, on a third, a shivering puppy, looking out at the field and the woods beyond.

He felt angry and wanted to rescue the poor little thing. And he looked at the house where, on New Year's Eve, he'd seen Aunt Mari with the shadowy man, the one his dad thought was a money launderer. There he was *again* – and there was someone talking to him. It was Aunt Mari again. He could almost touch her.

Robbie put his hand in his pocket and pulled out a potato. He ate it slowly while he thought.

Hadn't his mum and her friend whispered something about Aunt Mari's boyfriend? He'd heard the word 'investigator'. Maybe it was true. But what was he investigating? He would have to find out.

The next day, after school, he cycled up to the arts centre. He arrived feeling excited. He'd decided to confide in Julie and tell her everything. He could hardly wait. He walked up to the door full of anticipation. Then he saw the notice: CLOSED. Of course, it was Monday. Dejected, he got on his bike and turned towards home. He realised he didn't know where Julie lived, but then remembered... Rehearsal! It was happening tonight.

Dad said yes! I never thought he would. He doesn't like the show and he usually says no to everything. I was at Aunt Mari's when Mum came to tell me. I went straight home to see if he was there yet. My bike flew along, down the hill, faster than a rocket. I was speeding through the air and I did a few jumps too. Dad was home. I do love him, I gave him a hug. He liked it. He was smiling! At least, I thought he was. But then he told me that I must be very careful as there are all sorts of dangerous people in the show. Who are they, I wonder?

CHAPTER 8

Another detective

Robbie watched his mum making supper. She was chopping a bunch of mint. The silvery, watery smell filled the warm kitchen. Robbie knew his mum had been trying hard to cook special meals since his dad agreed to their being in the show.

She began to tell him a story, one Robbie knew well. His mum had been brought up in the countryside with her two sisters, and in their kitchen garden were blackcurrant bushes which gave off a dark, foxy smell, and beyond that a sort of wilderness where there were swathes of mint which, when crushed underfoot, released a magnificent scent. There was her eldest sister Lizzie, then Mari, and lastly his mum.

Her father had worked as estate manager on the huge Lough Barren Estate. He'd been a kind man and very musical. The three of them had sometimes sang with their dad.

When his mum was eight, her father was killed chopping down a rotten tree on the estate, so the three girls never had a chance to say their goodbyes. But his love of music and singing was passed on to his mum.

'I miss all that music and singing we did, it got lost somewhere,' she said. 'Let's hope this musical will bring it back.'

I'm at my first rehearsal. Some of the children look nice,

but I wish Julie was here, because I get on all right with her. I'm feeling a bit sick standing here with all the other singers. I expect it'll be all right when we start, because it will be like choir practice.

Miss Shirley is playing the intro, and SP is handing out song sheets and telling us to look at her because she's counting in time. One and two and three and four. Here we go. '*Somewhere Over the Rainbow*.' I haven't got a song sheet, and I don't know the words.

I'm standing next to the girl with long hair who sang before me. Maddy. She wants to share her song sheet with me.

The empty hall grew warmer as the voices of the new choir started to come together and fill it with sound and the singers' cheeks began to glow. His mum was singing with others, her voice flying high. Robbie soon felt a new strength in his voice and, without even noticing it, stopped feeling anxious.

On the third night of rehearsals Robbie again stood next to the long-haired Maddy, and as they whispered together he realised that they were getting on. After that, they sought each other out and stood side by side, always sharing song sheets when there weren't enough to go round. Robbie learned that Maddy went to school with some of the boys in the chorus, including a pair of boy twins, and he'd spent some time chatting with them.

Robbie wanted to see Julie, so he decided he'd go up to the arts centre after school the following day.

He found her in conversation with Rory O'Connor. She was wearing her white dungarees and had a little hairband with rosebuds on it. Robbie felt pleased to have such a flamboyant friend when everyone else went out and about in such dull clothes all the time.

She winked at him as he stood by the shipwreck exhibit, examining the photos of the *Princess Victoria* before the wreck, and when Rory O'Connor had gone back upstairs to his sanctuary, she took him into her office, a little room behind the front desk, and offered him a cup of tea.

Robbie was feeling very much at home at the arts centre as well as at the Carrick Hall; both were places he really liked going to. Better in some ways than lying in the woods under his tree, and certainly warmer.

The telephone rang; Julie quickly sat down at the switchboard hidden behind the reception desk. He heard her say, 'Mr O'Connor is out, I'm afraid, can I help you?'

Robbie heard what sounded at first like the yapping of a terrier, but was in reality an angry voice. He thought he heard the terrier say, 'Tell him he'd bloody well better shape up or—'

At this point Julie noticed he was listening and waved him away. He went into the entrance hall and couldn't hear the rest of the conversation. But he moved back; being a detective, he didn't want to miss anything. She was picking up another call.

'Arlen Arts Centre, can I help you?'

'This is Rebecca Jones of the *Arlen Post*,' said a voice so sharp and piercing that Robbie could hear every word. 'I'm doing a feature on the musical show your director's putting on at the Carrick Hall. I'd like to come over and interview Mr O'Connor and discuss the role that the arts centre plays in our city.'

Julie said, 'I'm afraid the director's in a meeting right now. Could you ring back in an hour, do you think?'

Julie beckoned Robbie into her snug office behind the reception desk, and left him eating biscuits while she went upstairs to have a word with the director. Deciding to do a bit more detective work, Robbie crept up the stairs behind her and peeped over the top step into Rory O'Connor's office.

O'Connor was seated behind his desk in the centre of a pleasant, airy room filled with bookshelves and armchairs. Robbie was impressed by a coloured painting of a yellow snake which hung over the mantelpiece of a large fireplace. A very big window looked out over the port, a mile or so below.

On the windowsill lay a pair of scuffed, long-range binoculars. In one of the chairs Robbie could see half a figure, a man with a ruddy face and rough grey hair. His face was turned away. As he watched, the man's head began to turn towards him, as if he realised someone was there. Robbie bobbed down, but he just had time to recognise the sad-looking brown eyes – like a spaniel's, he thought. It was Aunt Mari's boyfriend!

'I can watch the whole port from here, O'Connor,' he said. 'It's a lot more comfortable than camping out in my car. I'm most grateful to you.'

When Robbie looked at Rory O'Connor's face he was

scowling, as if he wasn't pleased about having someone else in his office. Perhaps it distracted him from his work.

Quietly, Robbie tiptoed back downstairs. He heard Julie talking to the two men as she came out of the upstairs room; quickly, he sat down and picked up a biscuit. He suddenly had a lot to think about.

CHAPTER 9

Fishing for information

It was a bright cold day. Already rehearsals had been going on for a week and the singers were really on form. Tonight would be the first session with the choir and the dancers together on the stage.

Robbie woke before his parents were up. He made himself a quick breakfast, which he ate standing up, and shouted up the stairs, 'Just going out for a bike ride.'

But when he went to get his bike, the chain had gone. Annoyed, he took the chain off his dad's bike, which had flat tyres and was never used. He managed to fit it on OK, but ended up covered in black grease.

The morning was getting off to a bad start.

Eventually, he was ready to go and he pedalled down to the dock to see the fishermen.

Sandy and his partner Scott were on the quay with a catch of gurnard still jumping in the hold. The fish had big, round eyes, armour-plated heads, spiky spines, and feelers everywhere. Gleaming red, orange and gold, they looked to Robbie like a hatch of baby dragons in the sunlight. He parked his bike for a closer look.

'Hey there, Robbie,' said Sandy. His cheeks were glowing as he worked in the sunshine. He took off his yellow mackintosh and started piling up some faded blue and red plastic boxes ready for the catch.

'We cooked the lobster, and it went red,' said Robbie. 'It was very good. They said thank you.'

Sandy gave him a big smile. 'Right you are, glad you enjoyed it. It's as good as it gets, fresh lobster. By the way, you know your cousin; Jeff, is he called? We spotted him with that wee bloke from down south – the dancer.'

Robbie tried not to look interested.

'Where did you see him?' he said, bending over to pick some fish scales off his shoe.

'It was late last night. They were down in that old Ifflick Bar on the dock,' he said, pointing along to the quay beyond the fishing boats. 'It's a bit of a deadbeat place, like. Rough. I sometimes sing there and I went in for a warm-up.'

'Was he all right?' said Robbie anxiously. 'You know, Jeff?'

A small scruffy brown dog came up and sniffed at the pile of nets on the quay.

'I'd say so,' said Sandy, starting to sort the gurnard and chucking them into the coloured boxes. 'Very noticeable pair they were, him so tall and the other one so short.' He scratched the dog behind the ear. 'Hello Buster,' he said.

Another fisherman came over to join the conversation.

'They've been having a jar there just about every night this week,' he said. 'You'd think that smart little feller could find somewhere better, but there's always plenty craic in there.'

'Maybe they're waiting for someone to turn up,' replied Sandy.

The two men were now talking across Robbie and forgetting he was there. He bent to pet the scruffy terrier.

'Something's going on, if you ask me, with Jeff these days. First taking himself off, and now he's back, splashing his cash,' said Sandy.

Robbie took note.

CHAPTER 10

The gang

In the 1940s it was common knowledge that the Nazis planned to invade Britain and annexe London, as they had annexed Paris. Winston Churchill and his staff remained in Whitehall but a secret emergency War Office was built for him to retreat to with his War Cabinet – if the time came.

The remote site chosen was across the water from Arlen on the west coast of Scotland, squatting low in the green coastal landscape like a fortress; a vast grey concrete complex of underground corridors and large dark rooms. After the war it was decommissioned and the utility furniture and tin filing cabinets were sold off. Someone bought the concrete shell and blocked off most of the doorways with cement, turning the rooms into giant seawater tanks for holding live shellfish.

The crustaceans came in on small fishing boats and were transferred from the loading bay into oxygenated tanks. These would be transported on larger ships, many bound for Spain.

One of the smaller fishing boats bringing in the shellfish was the *Santa Fay*. Sandy and Scott had Robbie on board. They'd asked his mum if they could treat him to a boat trip and she'd agreed. The fishermen were familiar with this strange, cold place, which was called simply 'the bunker'.

Tomorrow was Sunday, and Sandy and Scott wanted to

offload their live, jostling catch of lobsters and Dublin Bay prawns as fast as possible and then get themselves back over to Arlen, which was only a few miles away over the water.

Following them into the bunker from the bright February afternoon Robbie paused in the dim light, brought up short by the relative darkness; it was a sombre, echoey place.

As they wheeled in the trolley filled with boxes of live shellfish, they heard the hollow sound of footsteps in a distant corridor, but when their eyes had adjusted to the gloom and they turned into the main part of the building, there was no one there.

They took the catch to the central office and weighing station, which was lit by the pale glare of neon tubes. They knocked on the window and the manager – sunny in yellow waterproof trousers and a Fair Isle sweater – appeared, looking sleepy.

'You got company today, Jazzer? We heard someone around.'

Jazzer had his radio playing and hadn't heard anything. Scott and Sandy shrugged and Jazzer helped them weigh their catch and empty the crustaceans into Tank 5. This done, they headed back to their boat and set off across the North Channel for home.

That night at the Carrick Hall, the dancers and singers were together on a crowded stage. Windy was deciding where everyone should go. Robbie watched him as he bounced around, ordering little groups of people to stand here or wait there and making marks on the floor with chalk. Robbie was puzzled. Windy knew Jeff well; he met him for drinks in a scruffy bar. What were they doing together? Maybe the fishermen were right; they were waiting for someone – or something – to arrive on one of the boats. Or maybe they were just having a chat. He decided he must find out. And soon.

I might have a chance to find Jeff now. I'd like to have a look at that bar where Scott and Sandy saw Jeff with Windy. I wish I knew what they were up to. I want to go down there after the rehearsal, but not on my own. I need someone else. Maybe Maddy – but I'll have to tell Mum I'm going for a sleepover, so I'd better ask the twins too. It would be better if we all go together. We can say we're on our way home from rehearsals if anyone asks. Jeff would recognise me, but he doesn't know them so they can keep a watch on Jeff if we find him.

Having decided to see what his friends in the cast would think about going on a mission with him to the Ifflick Bar, Robbie sat down next to Maddy during the break and started to explain.

'I'm watching Windy,' he said, 'because he seems to know my cousin Jeff who's run away from home.'

'How old is Jeff?' asked Maddy.

'He's seventeen,' said Robbie. 'He left school and then he kind of disappeared. But I've heard he's been seen a few times in a bar on the docks and that's where he meets Windy. I'd like to go there, but it's out of bounds.'

'That sounds exciting,' said Maddy. The two of them exchanged glances and their eyes were shining.

They talked to the twins, Charlie and Harry – who was there to watch his twin brother, although he hadn't made it into the choir himself – who listened with mounting enthusiasm.

Robbie briefed them. 'We are detectives, and we're trying to find out why Windy keeps meeting my cousin Jeff who has run away from home. I want to find Jeff. They go to a scruffy place called the Ifflick Bar on the quay, beyond the fishing boats, so we need to go there.'

'But what if our parents come in and see us?' said Maddy.

'Don't worry,' said Robbie. 'Sandy, my friend who's a fisherman, says it's a rough place. Your parents wouldn't be seen dead in there.'

'What was Windy doing in a place like that?' said Charlie.

'That's what we want to find out,' said Robbie.

'I'll tell my mum and dad that I'm having a sleepover with my friend Flora,' said Maddy.

So in the end there were four of them, and the secret plan was made.

Windy was shouting, 'And dodge and back, and dodge and back, keep those shoulders down, darlings! And now fall into each other's arms.' The dancers embraced each other. Robbie wondered what his mum was thinking when Rafferty clasped his arms round the pink-haired girl in front of him, dressed in a leopard onesie. The leopard, Julie, her head tilted back, smiled up at Rafferty.

While Robbie and his fellow singers sang their parts to

the playing of Miss Shirley, they were casting sideways glances along the row. When they'd finished rehearsing, they went to find their parents and gave them the excuses they'd cooked up. They intended to creep back into their homes later, pretending there'd been a quarrel at the sleepover and they'd chosen to come home after all. They went off in pairs, after making sure that their parents didn't bump into each other.

The air was dry and sharp. The little group gathered outside in the dimly lit street and set off for the dock together, marching along under the yellow street lights. Charlie had a torch with him in case they needed it.

They got to the dock; the ships loomed up blackly over them and they breathed in the reek of fish, seaweed and petrol that constantly hung in the air of the fishing quays. Their footsteps echoed on the empty dock.

'Remember, if anyone asks us what we're doing,' said Robbie, 'we must all say we're on our way home from rehearsals.'

'What shall we do if we find them? Shall we follow Windy?' asked Maddy.

'We might get into trouble if we got caught doing that,' said Robbie, 'but we can follow Jeff and find out where he's staying.'

'Exactly how are we going to do this?' said Harry.

The twins decided that Robbie couldn't just go into the bar and pretend to be looking for his father or something, because everybody knew Mr Laggan wasn't the sort of person to go near such a place.

'No one knows me, or knows that my parents wouldn't go

in there,' said Maddy. 'So I could pretend to be looking for my dad. But I don't know what Jeff looks like.'

'Like a punk,' said Harry, which set them giggling. They decided on a plan.

Robbie would creep into the bar. If he was careful, he could see Jeff without letting Jeff see him.

'What if he sees us following him?' said Harry.

'Let's take it in turns to track him, so when he turns round it will always be someone different. What do you think?' said Charlie.

'Yes, but how do we know who to follow?' said Harry.

'I can give a sign when he comes out, wave my scarf,' said Robbie.

Ifflick's Bar could be heard roaring out long before it came into view. From the outside it was a low, dumpy building, a run-down, dirty place. Grimy doors and windows, painted a crusty dark red, were splashing light on to concrete covered with rubbish.

In front, a couple of large barrels, standing on the cobbles, stood in for tables. Two bony, weather-beaten old men with blond hair sat on a bench. The first had red-rimmed eyes, and the other seemed to have a gammy leg, which stuck out in front of him. A beery waft came from the door, along with the barrage of loud voices. To the little gang, it did not look inviting – but it *did* look intriguing.

Robbie looked at the others.

'Go on, Robbie, go on, we can't stop now,' they whispered.

'I'm going in,' he said, 'but if I'm not back in ten minutes, come and look for me.'

'We will, we will,' they said, and with his woolly hat pulled well down and his collar up, shoulders hunched, hands in pockets, into the half-light roar he went.

He slid around the wall, as close as he could, scanning the faces. He looked at the bunch of people propping up the bar, mainly red-faced heavily built men. Robbie recognised a few faces as dock workers or local lorry drivers, dressed in their work clothes, multi-coloured waterproofs and high-vis jackets. All were drinking treacle-black stout, much of it slopped out on the bar top.

Then he held his breath – there was Windy, tucked into a low table over in the far corner! He had two half-empty drinks in front of him. Robbie watched and waited, half concealed behind a cabinet full of packets of crisps.

From his dark corner, he saw Jeff making his way to the table; he finished his drink without sitting down, leaned over and said something to Windy who smiled up at him.

The babbling hum of the bar was suddenly shattered by shouts and cries coming from outside and everyone started to rush to the door. From a nearby window Robbie saw the two gaunt old men from the bench and his three friends thrashing around on the ground, trying to hang on to a young fellow, holding him by the arms and the legs, by the coat, by the ears – anywhere they could get hold of him. He, in turn, was on top of a tall young man who was squirming under the flailing arms and legs, face down on the filthy pavement. There were shouts of 'Stop him!' and 'Get hold of him!' and 'Help!'

Robbie ran outside and immediately recognised the man they were rescuing as Julie's friend Rafferty, his mum's dance partner.

Deserting the bar, people hurried to help and collared the youngster, who was gabbling, 'It was him, it was him!' and pointing at Rafferty.

'He started it!' he yelled as he was dragged out of the heap of children pinning him down.

Two beefy lads grabbed the young thug on either side and marched him off down the street. Rafferty got up and dusted himself off, looking sheepish; he didn't see Robbie. He had a grazed cheek. He was holding up his right elbow with his left hand, and they saw that some of his fingers were sticking out at a strange angle.

'We got him!' said Harry, dancing in the road, fired up with excitement.

'We caught him, he was going to punch that man. I think he was trying to mug him,' said Maddy. Robbie felt quite left out because it hadn't been him, but he was glad they'd had an adventure and collared a crook. Rafferty took himself off to get his broken fingers fixed. Then Robbie remembered their mission and rushed back into the bar.

Jeff and Windy were gone.

The rest of the children followed him into Ifflick's and some of the bystanders cheered them and bought them crisps and lemonade. People all seemed very friendly and the children enjoyed the sensation of being heroes for a minute. The two old men from outside were invited in and given a glass of ale.

'Would you not make that a whiskey?' demanded the red-eyed man, somewhat imperiously. There was laughter, the atmosphere became raucous again and the children were forgotten, so they started off for home.

CHAPTER 11

Rehearsing

Robbie's Uncle Martin had been asked to do the scenery for the performance – he was known to be good at DIY – while Aunt Mari had been put in charge of costumes. Most of the young ones who were in the play would be dressed as plants in a flower shop. Aunt Mari was sitting at her kitchen table, her sewing machine going like the clappers with reams of green net flying over the table when Robbie called round on Sunday morning.

Thanks to the buzzing of the gossip hive, she already knew about Robbie's outing with the gang the previous night. And the attack on Rafferty. She knew that they'd saved Rafferty from a mugger and that he'd been injured.

It seemed that the lads who'd carted the mugger off had soon let him go, partly because they didn't want to be inside a police station themselves, but also because they'd found out who he was – Rafferty's younger brother, Terry.

Aunt Mari looked at Robbie over the top of her spectacles.

'So what were you doing last night at Ifflick's Bar, may I ask?'

Robbie looked as unconcerned as he could.

'Oh, you know, we were just going by on the way to our sleepovers,' he said.

Aunt Mari held up a fluffy green skirt and shook it out, placing it on a pile of green frills.

'I'm not going to say anything this time,' she said, picking up another frilly skirt, 'but you want to be careful, Robbie. There's plenty that don't like their young children out at night, especially in the winter – and in that seedy place! Your dad is one of them.'

'We were all together,' he said, which was almost true. 'It was lucky we were there! We helped rescue Rafferty.'

Aunt Mari pursed her lips and shook her head. 'Listen to me. You'll get yourself in trouble, Robbie, if you don't watch out.'

Robbie was exhilarated by the Sunday rehearsal. The choir was really coming together, although mistakes were still being made. SP made fun of them and mimicked them, showing them how stiffly they stood, how wooden they appeared, like a row of puppets with no joints. But, encouraged to copy her example, they soon found themselves swinging their hips and swaying to her relaxed rhythm.

She wanted everything moving: arms in the air, bracelets tinkling, fingers snapping. Robbie felt he was making an idiot of himself at first, but gradually began to get the idea. They weren't *supposed* to be themselves; they had to pretend to be someone else, someone American. Slowly he relaxed and, under her hand, he kept trying until it felt right. The others were loosening up too and soon they looked like a happy, swinging chorus line rather than a row of awkward novices. She made them applaud each other.

The dancers started to dance. Things often went wrong, ending in frustration and instructions to repeat. Rafferty was there with his hand bound up and a scorching red mark on his cheek. Windy, wearing a little woolly beanie and leg warmers, was beating out the rhythm and giving everyone a hard time.

Because it got dark early, and was cold and raining so hard that the gutters were overflowing – not to mention homework and the prospect of getting up early to go to school the next day – the gang didn't manage to get near the Ifflick Bar again during the whole of that week.

Rehearsals continued well and Robbie could see the fast and funny musical starting to take shape. The scene is set in a dingy run-down flower shop. Seymour, the downtrodden shop assistant, played by Rafferty, is in love with the florist, Audrey, played by Julie in a bright yellow dress. Audrey already has a boyfriend, a sadistic dentist who treats her cruelly. But she's secretly in love with Seymour.

Robbie's mum was playing one of the chorus of ladies in tight pink dresses who help ramp up the tension as a new plant winds its tendrils through the little flower shop. But this is no ordinary plant. It is a plant with a mouth, a whingeing, hungry plant, played by Windy, who would be swathed in reams of green and pink ruffles. The plant, it transpires, is a man-eater.

The actual performance in front of a live audience would be the following Saturday. On Friday evening there would be a dress rehearsal and their costumes were ready to try. The gang resolved to visit the Ifflick Bar again after the final rehearsal.

CHAPTER 12

Friday the thirteenth

At lunchtime Robbie's mum put some baked potatoes and salad on the kitchen table. Robbie was hungry after being outside in the freezing wind. His school was shut for the day thanks to a broken boiler and the classrooms deemed to be too cold.

Robbie's dad had come home for lunch unexpectedly, and sat there brooding and silent, his face unshaven and dark with chagrin.

'Why aren't you at the Bear with your mates?' asked his mum.

'It seems nobody wants to see me any more since that business at the hall,' he muttered. Robbie saw him bite his lower lip quite hard. He looked smouldering, ready to burst into flames, and Robbie guessed he was holding in his anger.

'Why don't you come tonight to the dress rehearsal and you can hear Robbie sing,' suggested his mum.

His dad looked as if he was about to say no, but she went on in a coaxing tone.

'You can tell Rory O'Connor about your mistake – I'm sure he'll understand. He's very nice and very easy to talk to.'

His dad inspected his fork for a moment and then threw it down. Robbie wondered what was coming.

'All right, if that's what you want.' He leaned back in his chair. 'It probably couldn't make matters any worse.'

After lunch, when his dad had gone back to work, Robbie called out to his mum, 'Just going for a bike ride.'

'OK,' she said, 'don't stay out too long, we mustn't be late for dress rehearsal, and I want you to have your tea before we go.'

As Robbie left the house and started to push his bike over the pavement and on to the road, a man walked past and suddenly stumbled into the bike, knocking Robbie over. The passer-by didn't stop. In fact, by the time Robbie picked himself and his bike up, the man had strode rapidly on and was almost out of sight. Robbie continued to the woods and settled down under his tree to investigate his own house and the one belonging to Aunt Mari's secret boyfriend.

That was funny, that man barging straight into me like that. He wasn't sorry and I think he meant to do it. I wonder why. Hang on, what's this? There's something sticking out of my coat pocket. It's an envelope. It wasn't there before. It must be from him. What can it be?

Friday 13th
I need your help.
Meet me down by the *Santa Fay*
at 3.30 p.m. sharp.

It must be from Jeff. I wonder why that man didn't stop to give it to me. It's very mysterious. I'll get Charlie and

Harry to come with me. Isn't Friday the thirteenth always supposed to be unlucky?

Robbie made his way over to Charlie and Harry's house. But they went to a different school which, of course, had no broken boiler and so they weren't at home. Their mum answered and introduced herself as Fay, asking him if she could help. Robbie knew the twins got out of class early on Fridays, so he borrowed a pen and some paper from her and left a note for them.

> Important. Going to meet Jeff by the *Santa Fay*
> at 3.30. Please come down.
> Tell Maddy too.
> Robbie.

He folded it in half so Fay wouldn't see what he'd written. He hoped they'd come.

As the appointed time approached, Robbie went down to the fishing quay. The water heaved, oily and slick. The tide was up, the sky was clearing and it was getting colder. The ramshackle old boats were rocking in the swell, playing a metallic tune as the rigging cables hit the masts.

There was nobody around. Robbie wished his friends would turn up.

A stooped man came by, wearing a black hoodie.

'If you're Robbie,' he called out as he hobbled along the

quay, 'I expect you'll find who you're looking for on that boat there, the blue one.'

There was a blue motor boat tied up at the jetty, between two fishing boats. Robbie went to inspect it. It was called, rather oddly, *Blue Fairy*.

He climbed on board and ducked down into the cabin. A hunched figure wrapped in a blanket shot out a scrawny arm and pulled him inside, clutching Robbie with strong bony fingers. It certainly wasn't Jeff. He could hardly tell if it was a man or a woman, but he caught a glimpse of pale eyes with red drooping lids.

'You wait in here with me. I'll make yer a hot drink,' muttered the figure, slamming the door of the small cabin, and filling a mug from the kettle. Robbie watched as the sinister figure added a couple of spoons of hot-chocolate powder, some sugar and something which Robbie assumed was milk powder. Robbie took the steaming mug that was handed to him.

'You! Sit on that bench,' wheezed his captor. 'Get in behind the table, and drink.'

Robbie shuddered. Without thinking, he sipped the hot chocolate. He was hoping against hope that Charlie and Harry would get here very soon. But even if they did, they wouldn't know where he was. He gently squeezed out from behind the table and made a dash for the door of the cabin. He'd just managed to open it and get half out of the door when the man with the black hoodie who he'd seen on the quay jumped on board, with surprising agility, and pushed him back into the cabin. The controls of the boat were winking their little lights. The man sat down, grabbed the steering gear and started the motor.

'Where's Jeff? Who are you? Let me out of here!' cried Robbie.

The words started to jumble around in his head and lose their meaning. The man began to look a little blurred. He thought maybe the man was taking him out to sea, but he struggled to focus.

'Stop, help!' he wanted to shout, but no sound came out. He saw his red-eyed captor grinning. The boat was moving now, but Robbie was falling; he felt darkness take over as he slumped face down on the little table in front of him.

When Robbie came to, he tried to think what to do, but he could hardly tell which way up he was. The effect of the spiked chocolate was only now wearing off. He'd never really got to see the kidnappers properly before he'd passed out. He'd been tricked and walked straight into their trap. He knew, with frantic certainty, that he had to get out. But all he could remember was that he'd vaguely heard them talking as they dragged him off the boat.

When he finally lifted his heavy eyelids, a sickly greenish light revealed his predicament. He was in a small, square room. On all four sides were windows looking out on to blank darkness. He was lying painfully on a floor of cold cement which was none too clean and smelled strongly of stale fish. He heard approaching voices and decided to pretend that he was still knocked out cold.

The room was soon echoing to the noise of the drunken chat of two men. Robbie could smell cigarette smoke and it sounded as though the men were swigging something out of a bottle. Slowly, Robbie opened his eyes a little. These men were the two from the boat. They looked as though they'd been left out in the sun too long. Underneath their blond hair, their freckled skin looked shrivelled and wrinkled. Their teeth gleamed white, which looked odd in their haggard faces. With a jolt, Robbie recognised them as the two old men from outside the Ifflick Bar – one with the red eyes and one with a gammy leg.

'I was gutted when I lost that house,' said the one with the red eyes, laughing. 'But now – get this – at my new villa the swimming pool will be immense, bigger than yours even.' He took another gulp from his bottle. 'It's high time I had a proper pool after all the risks I've taken.'

'Pity you can't swim then, isn't it?' said the other, cackling. 'Better not have a deep end or you might fall in and drown yerself.'

'Very funny. But don't forget where I'll be this time tomorrow,' said Red Eye. 'I'll be getting off that plane and stepping out in the heat with a wad in my bag big enough to buy the whole airport.'

'Then we could *really* do some business, if you owned the airport, Mel!' said Gammy Leg.

The sound of a groan came from the floor. Robbie played possum but peered through lowered eyelids. It was Jazzer! The manager of the bunker was lying at their feet, tied up with a gag over his mouth.

'I wish that little gobshite Terry would hurry up and bring the readies,' said Red Eye, giving Jazzer a push with his foot. 'I'm going get nervous if we have to wait much longer. And when I get nervous, I get nasty.'

'Is the boat ready? Crabs and lobsters loaded? Gotta look like a normal fishing boat if we're stopped.'

'All ready,' confirmed Red Eye.

They must be smugglers, whiling away the time while they waited for the cash for their cargo! Robbie reasoned that smugglers wouldn't unload their cargo until they were paid, so all they could do was wait. Whatever their cargo was, it must be valuable if the man could buy a house with a swimming pool.

The men stopped talking and Robbie could hear footsteps. One of the men flung open the door and dragged a younger man into the room. So this must be Terry with the readies. He looked familiar, but Robbie couldn't place him and it was hard to see properly in the gloom.

Terry took off a bulging backpack and emptied a mass of tightly packed bundles on to Jazzer's desk.

Robbie held his breath – so much money. The two old men looked at each other triumphantly, grinning.

'What happens now?' said Terry.

'We'll motor the trawler to Arlen just after dawn,' said Red Eye.

'The wind's dropped and it's going to be pretty calm tonight. Should be an easy crossing,' said Gammy Leg. 'What d'you want to do with the boy?'

'We'll lock him up here until tomorrow,' said Red Eye

in a cold voice. 'This one too,' he continued, aiming a kick at poor Jazzer, 'but in a separate room. You'd better go and ring Laggan.'

That almost made Robbie sit up. Laggan! His name. And they were going to lock him up overnight. Was there no one around who could save him? And why were they ringing his dad?

'What shall I say to him?'

'Just tell him you've got his brat and he can't have him back unless he turns a blind eye to the shipment going to Arlen port tonight – he'll know what you're on about!'

Gammy Leg turned and left. Red Eye was laughing quietly.

'We've got him now. We'll be able to come and go as often as we like. Once Laggan's helped us tonight, he won't dare say no again.'

'Not if he knows what's good for him ... and his boy,' sneered Terry.

The two men dragged Robbie, still pretending to be out cold, along a corridor full of wet noise, of splashing and trickling and dripping. They dumped him like a bin bag on the floor and left, arguing about the best place to put Jazzer for the night.

Robbie crouched, shivering, in the corner of another dank, twilit concrete room that stank of shellfish and cement, listening to splashes, splatters and drips. He'd never felt so scared, so miserable, so frozen and hollow. Or so alone. There was no escape – he could make out only the dimmest of lights coming from a square hole, high up in the wall. And he'd heard the key turn in the lock as his captors left. Cold drops fell on him from the ceiling. The damp and the mould were getting into his bones.

He sat on the wet floor trembling, like the puppy he'd seen shut out on the balcony. He hunched himself into a ball to keep a spark of warmth in his chilled body. Now he could hear stronger-sounding ripples and splashes. His fear increased. Could the tide fill the chamber?

Robbie started, suddenly alert; he could hear a new sound, the low-gear throb of an engine in the distance, but coming closer. There was a rumble, sounds of huge doors creaking, a cacophony of metallic crashes, cascading water and the rasping and running of metal chains, all echoing in and around Robbie's prison.

That noise sounded like a boat. My head is less woozy, I'm starting to think straight, and I know what my dad would expect. He'd want me to be strong and brave. I will try, but I still feel a bit weak and shaky. But I must try to get rescued. I can't just sit here; if there are boats then there's someone about. They might help me...

Robbie stood up. 'Somebody let me out, somebody get me out!' he shouted over and over, making his voice as loud as he could. He called and called. At last, he heard an echoing sound – footsteps!

In the hole high up in the wall there appeared a face, like a pale waxwork. Robbie shrank into the corner, fearing it was one of his captors. Then to his joy, he found he knew the face – it was Charlie! He waved an arm from the window and gave Robbie the thumbs up through the hole. Putting a finger to his lips, he disappeared. Relief swept through Robbie; Charlie and Harry were on the case. But how on earth had they found him...?

Harry and Charlie had read Robbie's note and gone straight to the docks without trying to contact Maddy; Robbie's note had sounded urgent and they wanted to get there fast.

They'd been just in time to see a stooped man in a black hoodie jumping hurriedly on to a blue motor boat and pushing someone back into the cabin. The boat was turning and heading out of the harbour.

'Whoever that man pushed back into the cabin, they were small. I think it must be Robbie,' said Charlie. 'I think he may have been trying to escape when the man shoved him back inside.'

'Oh, God!' said Harry. 'He's been kidnapped. It must be Jeff! He and Windy must have clocked him watching them in that bar and that's why they disappeared.'

'What should we do?' said Charlie.

'Let's tell someone,' said Harry. 'But who?'

They caught sight of Sandy and Scott who were loading the chiller hold of the *Santa Fay* with boxes of ice. Robbie had mentioned this boat in his note, so they ran over.

'Can you help us?' said Charlie. 'Our friend Robbie has just been taken in that blue motor boat, the one called the *Blue Fairy*.'

'We think he's been kidnapped,' said Harry, 'by his cousin.'

Charlie and Harry had been in luck; Scott and Sandy had listened to their story, understood at once that Robbie was in danger and hurried the twins on board. They set off in pursuit of the *Blue Fairy* at speed. They could see from the wake she left behind which direction to follow. After a few miles they were well up behind the blue boat, and could see it was on course for the bunker. To avoid being spotted, they pretended to be on another route, as if just passing by on the way to Cairnryan. They didn't want the kidnappers to suspect they were being followed.

The sky was almost dark when they arrived at the bunker. They saw the *Blue Fairy* moored outside, but the boat was empty.

Sandy and Scott crept along the corridor between the lobster tanks, the twins behind them. There was no sign of Jazzer at his desk in the central office and no sound from his radio. The only noises were watery drips and splashes that resonated like underwater music in the hushed, dank space. They tiptoed forwards, listening intently for any human sound. All they could hear were far-off, muffled, birdlike cries.

'I thought I heard something, it could've been a kittiwake,' said Sandy.

'There it is again,' said Scott. They turned and crept towards the noise which, as they came closer, sounded more human – could it be...?

They followed the cries to a dim, rank-smelling cement corridor, with green algae growing halfway up the walls. Faint, anaemic strip lights hung from the ceiling. They illuminated a small window, only just visible in the shadows, high up in the wall. The shouts were coming from in there. But the door was padlocked. Sandy got Charlie up on his shoulders to look through the tiny window.

Robbie was there, just visible in the corner of the dim chamber.

Sandy smashed the padlock off the door to the cell with a monkey wrench from the *Santa Fay* tool kit. They knew time might be short and their first priority was to get Robbie – who was shivering, soaked through and blue with cold – out of this hole and away to safety.

Robbie walked on unsteady legs towards the twins. Scott took off his yellow oilskin jacket and wrapped it round Robbie, who was trying hard not to cry with relief at seeing his friends. He wanted to laugh instead, but it came out as a snort. Charlie, always the comedian, copied him, giving a louder snort. In a moment they were all snorting and laughing from sheer relief. They fell silent as the sound of rasping chains came from the direction of the loading dock. Robbie stood still, his mind flashing with images of being grabbed by that bony hand.

'It was those two old men from outside the Ifflick Bar,' he whispered. 'They tricked me. They must still be here somewhere. There's something going on, I heard them talking about it. And they've got Jazzer gagged and bound in another room somewhere.'

Robbie told them of the strange sounds coming from the

far end of the building. Sandy and Scott were familiar with the place, and Robbie and the twins were desperate to find out what was going on. They sneaked their way to the end of the bunker, calling for Jazzer when they dared, but received no response. Eventually they came to the deepwater loading bay, silent except for the sighing sound of the dark water as it rose and fell.

They peered round the misty sheet of transparent plastic that covered the opening into the dock like a shroud. What on earth was glimmering in the deep water below the dock?

The humped shape of a submarine, silvery and sleek as a seal, lay rocking gently beneath them on black ripples. Whatever was going on here, Robbie knew that just seeing this sinister little vessel was asking for trouble.

'We need to go,' said Sandy. 'Now.'

'Wait,' said Robbie. 'What about Jazzer? We can't leave him here.'

'Sandy's right,' said Scott. 'We might look for hours and not find him, and if we get caught we're no use to him at all. The best thing we can do is get back to port and tell someone.'

They crept cautiously back to the *Santa Fay* and set off for home.

The sky had cleared. Anxious and watchful, they checked constantly to see if they were being followed. They didn't let down their guard until they saw the bulk of the Antrim Hills, black against the dark blue sky.

Still wrapped in Sandy's yellow fisherman's coat, Robbie stood on his own doorstep. Behind him were Scott, Sandy and the twins. He rang the bell.

It flew open and he saw the white haggard faces of his mum and dad lighting up with joy and relief. They got everyone inside.

'Sorry, Dad,' said Robbie. 'Hello, Mum.'

Soon his parents were offering Scott and Sandy warm drinks and food and the three boys were excitedly telling their story.

'I was drugged to the eyeballs, I thought I was a goner. It was sooo cold in there.'

'We saw you disappear into the boat when a man pushed you. It's lucky Scott and Sandy were there, we just followed the wake. They took a big risk to get you back,' said Charlie, with Harry nodding his agreement.

'It was scary seeing that submarine,' said Robbie. 'I'm glad there was no one around, it might have been curtains if anyone had seen us. But now we've got to help Jazzer.'

The doorbell rang.

'That'll be the police,' said Sandy. 'We rang them as soon as we got off the boat.'

Robbie's dad went to open the door. A figure, muffled against the cold, stepped in quietly.

'Good evening, good evening,' he said.

Robbie looked at his mum, who looked as confused as he felt.

'I'm Brendan Bentham – Detective Inspector Bentham,' he continued. 'I wonder if I could ask you a few questions?'

Robbie started as he recognised Aunt Mari's boyfriend. He looked at his father who was staring in silence. Again his dad had been wrong; he'd misjudged the man – not a swindling bookie, but someone high up in the police who was here to question them.

His dad told Bentham about the kidnapping and the threatening phone call. But it was the information the detective gathered from the boys and the two fishermen that was most enlightening. Mindful of Robbie's anxiety to help his fellow victim, Jazzer, Bentham set about making a plan.

Today will be something I remember for always. It ended OK but I've never been so scared before. That horrible place... It was lucky I left that note for Charlie and Harry. Thank goodness for them – and Sandy and Scott. If it hadn't been for them I'd still be there. I might've died. My teeth were chattering so hard I thought they'd break. Mum thought I should have a hot bath. The water felt stinging hot when I got in. I was so glad to get home. I'd thought I might not see Mum and Dad again.

I missed home so much when I was shut up there.

But it was a real thrill, seeing that silver submarine out there at the bunker. And knowing it belongs to smugglers...

Aunt Mari's boyfriend thought Sandy and Scott were all in on the plot, but I told him they were the ones who saved me. He questioned my dad too. After my bath I had a sandwich. Then it was my turn. I told him about the two old men and he got very interested.

He says I'm a key witness. I had to describe what they looked like, and tell him all about how I was kidnapped.

I told them about being knocked over with my bike and showed them the note I was given. He took it as evidence.

Dad said he'd been ordered by the smugglers to turn a blind eye to a particular boat's activities, or they'd give me a bad time. Well, actually, they did give me quite a bad time. I can't wait to tell Julie.

I hope they catch those crooks on the *Blue Fairy*. I'd like see them in handcuffs. And I hope Jazzer is OK.

We have to go to bed now. The twins have already told their mother they're staying over with me. It's the first time I've had friends for a sleepover.

And tomorrow it's *Little Shop of Horrors*!

But the night was not over.

'That submarine of yours,' Bentham told the boys as they were being ushered towards the stairs by Robbie's mum, 'is the key. Now we can go after them. We know these fast little subs can slip into the country unseen by hiding in the depths of the sea. They're made specifically for smuggling.'

'What was its cargo?' asked Robbie.

'We don't know yet,' replied Bentham. 'Those little machines are fast. You've got to be pretty cunning to catch them. I've sent the Marine Dive Unit boat from Stranraer to head them off. If it's OK with you, Mrs Laggan, I'd like to take the boys with me to watch the capture. Your husband told us the shellfish trawler they're using to land the cargo is due to dock in Arlen early this morning. So we need to leave now.'

Robbie saw his mum looking at him and the twins

uncertainly. She turned to Robbie's dad. 'What do you think? Shall we let them go?'

Robbie could see his dad was getting ready to say no, but Bentham broke in.

'I promise to bring them home safely, don't you worry. Get your coats, boys, wrap up warm.' Robbie could hear his dad starting to object, but they were already halfway out of the front door.

Some people appear to be weak on the outside, but have great inner strength – this was Bentham. Others appear strong on the outside, but inside they're weak. Robbie was starting to understand that his dad was such a man.

Two hours later Robbie and the twins, wearing life jackets and leaning on the rail of the coastguard launch, were anchored in dark waters close enough to the Scottish coast to see a trail of fast-moving red and white lights on a busy road a mile inland. They strained their eyes in the dark to watch as four black-clad, spiderlike figures slipped stealthily into the water from their mother ship, which lay beside them, a few hundred metres along the rocky shore from the bunker.

The swimmers were equipped with masks and oxygen cylinders and had a very large, steel-reinforced net with them, which they towed behind on floats. They were going fishing.

Sliding through the icy water, the deep-sea divers of the Marine Unit were making their way towards the bunker and its loading bay where a trawler was waiting, loaded with shellfish and, if their timing was right, the smuggled cargo from the sub.

In the dock of the bunker, beside the trawler, there was an eruption of bubbles in the water where the sub had been. Unseen, unheard, the four divers were swimming out of the dock, back towards their unit, holding fast to a steel cord. This cord was attached to a net with which they'd encircled the submarine.

Once they'd handed the hawser to the crew on board the mother ship, the sub would be carefully winched in, and towed back to base.

'OK, Jeff?' shouted one of the divers.

'OK, Keith,' came a voice that Robbie knew.

'Is that you, Jeff?' called Robbie.

'Hey, Robbie, what you doing here?'

'What are *you*?' replied Robbie.

'Just doing my job,' said Jeff, his voice fading as the divers' boat turned about and disappeared.

The coastguard launch entered the loading bay and nudged up to the trawler as the coastguards closed in on their prey.

Robbie and the twins weren't allowed on to the trawler. But they were wide awake and alert when three handcuffed captives were brought on board and locked up.

The boys wanted to know everything. Bentham sat in the galley with them and described the capture.

'The first thing we saw,' he said, 'were hundreds of lobsters, prawns and crabs crawling in green, bubbling, glass tanks. There was no one about. It seemed like a ghost ship, so we started to look for hiding places. We know all their tricks.'

'Where did you look?' said Charlie. 'I'd hide in the bilges, no one would find me there.'

'Well, they didn't think of that. We looked carefully at the wall of the cabin and found a false panel. The coastguards levered it off and inside we saw a lad and two older men crouching in that space by the chiller fan. As soon as we'd secured them, the coastguards went into the bunker to look for the manager. But we haven't found the cargo yet.

'We caught the lad fumbling in his coat pocket, and he started to pull out a gun, but the coastguards were too much for him. In their black bulletproof vests, they do look quite menacing. The poor lad was quaking. Luckily, he decided not to make things worse by pointing his pistol, so he tried to drop it behind him. I threw it overboard, and it lay floating on top of the waves. It was just a toy!'

A coastguard came in and whispered to Bentham.

'I won't be a moment,' he said as he went below.

When he came back he told them, 'One of the coastguards found the poor manager, still trussed up inside the bunker. He's resting down below. All he wanted was a hot cup of coffee. But he said he'd feared the cold would get him. Like you, Robbie! You had a lucky escape and you helped enormously, you and the boys – and Sandy and Scott, of course. We wouldn't have got here in time without you. Come on, let's get you three home.'

The dawn broke, the sky at first grey, misty, and then washed with a soft, peach pink. The colour gently blushed on the water. Beyond the soulless world of smuggling, the sunrise, as ever, was a reminder of the world's true beauty.

I saw Jeff just now. He came over to see us. He wanted to know what on earth we were doing on the coastguard's launch in the middle of the night.

I told him I'd been kidnapped and that Sandy and Scott and the twins had rescued me, and we'd found the silver submarine – and actually helped to capture the smugglers! They got those two horrible, ratty old men, and the younger one, who turned out to be Rafferty's younger brother, Terry. I knew there was something familiar about him… But after we saw the way he attacked his brother that night at the Ifflick Bar, I'm not surprised he was involved with a bad lot.

I nearly fell in the sea when I heard Jeff's voice on that dive boat – so that's what he's been up to! He isn't a diamond smuggler or a spy on the run – he's in the marine police, in something called the Dive Unit that helped capture our submarine.

Turns out, he has a friend who kept encouraging him to take the Marine Dive Unit's training course at Greenock and actually went and bought him the tickets to cross over to Scotland. So he just ran on to the next boat. That must be what was in the envelope I saw – so his friend is Windy Wake. He says this job is what he wants to do with his life. I think I'd tell my mum if I wanted to do something really badly, but he says he went and did his training secretly because the whole family is dead hostile to the police and he thought they'd stop him going. And he wasn't sure he'd pass the exams. He decided he'd best keep it quiet in case it all went wrong. But it didn't.

When he came to our house he was wearing a smart uniform and looked very pleased with himself. I asked him why he did all that birdwatching with me after Christmas and he said, 'Cousin, I like you. And I wondered what you were really up to. I was watching you watching me!' He laughed. He told me he'd enjoyed seeing me pretending to look at birds with my binoculars. 'I've got to hand it to you! You kept an eye on me, found me out at that Ifflick Bar.'

And we discovered that submarine. Well, it wasn't just me. But I was the one who went into the bar and found Jeff. I think I'm going to be a good detective!

CHAPTER 13

Not stealing

The twins were having a family get-together. They had a big family, so they'd hired entertainment to keep the children occupied while the adults chatted. The twins had invited Robbie along too. His mum had offered to make a cake – and regretted it immediately. She was a reluctant cook at the best of times. But then Robbie said he was happy to help.

'What kind of cake do you think the twins would like?' she asked him.

'They like carrot cake,' said Robbie. 'With cream cheese in the icing.'

He'd watched Fay making one once; she'd mentioned cream cheese and he'd made a mental note.

Together they went shopping, and together they baked the cake – they broke the eggs, beat the sugar with the sunflower oil and grated the carrots.

Robbie set off with their good-enough carrot cake. It wasn't a prize-winner, but it was a proper cake and they were proud of it.

The twins and Robbie were hanging back, lingering by the door, checking what the entertainment was before committing themselves to sitting down. After all, some of the children were a lot younger than they were.

The doorbell rang. Introducing herself as Mrs Marvella, a bulky woman in a shiny dress of black satin, came in carrying a bag and a couple of cat baskets. She opened the baskets and lifted out two snakes; a small yellow one looked particularly malevolent. Robbie and the twins sidled in and joined the group of awed children. This might be quite interesting after all.

Mrs Marvella, who smelled of cats, hadn't much to say about the reptiles, but Robbie liked the feel of the snake's muscular bodies and their cool dry firmness as the children took the creatures from each other very carefully and passed them round.

Mrs Marvella got a little box out of her bag, opened it and dipped in her fingers. Sitting on her palm was a hairy black spider over 7 centimetres across.

'Now, who wants to be photographed with Incy?' she said, holding out her hand. The spider, with swivelling eyes like black glass beads, looked around. It appeared docile until, like black lightning, it jumped off Mrs Marvella's hand on to the carpet. There was a shrill scream from Fay, and all the children jumped up. Pandemonium! The children all looked as if they were wearing shoes that were too tight and too big as they stumbled over one another trying to avoid the scurrying spider.

Mrs Marvella was down on all fours, lumbering about and attempting to catch the spider. Just as she was about to get hold of it, it scuttled away towards the window on velvety legs and climbed up the curtains. In an instant it was at head height. The twins tried to catch it in a large jar but it was too quick. Then Robbie thought of throwing a tea towel over it.

'Pesky thing,' said Mrs Marvella when Incy was back in the box. She picked up the snakes in their baskets and went out with them. Next she came back carrying a cage.

'Now you're going to meet Mr Ginger,' she said with what seemed to Robbie rather a fake smile on her face. She opened the cage and a small ginger-haired monkey, showing its teeth, put out a skinny arm and tried to pinch her. It looked terrified. She slammed the cage shut.

'Well, that's all for today, children,' said Mrs Marvella.

There were concerted cries of 'No!'

Robbie thought the monkey looked too thin.

'I think that monkey needs something to eat,' he said. Charlie produced a banana and soon Mr Ginger was sitting on the floor with the children, inspecting their ears and enjoying holding hands with them.

When Mrs Marvella eventually left, muttering under her breath, the monkey looked sadly at the children from its cage. Robbie had the distinct impression it wanted to stay.

Today is Sunday and I'm happy because the twins are coming over to my house. We asked Maddy too but she couldn't come. It's a pity because after lunch, which is pizza from the freezer, we're going to the place they call the Dark Hedges. I'm going to try actual birdwatching, so I'm taking my binoculars. It's near the quarry where they filmed that TV show. It's supposed to be haunted by the

Grey Lady, and at Halloween she summons all the ghosts from the nearby graveyard. It sounds a bit spooky.

It was great fun doing the show. But Dad wouldn't come to see it, so he never even heard me singing. We had a big party afterwards. We were all dressed up in our costumes. Everyone was there, and the twins and Maddy said we should do more detective stuff together.

We all decided that we like Scott and Sandy a lot. And I like it down on the quay. And we want to help them with the boat and the fishing and things. There's always lots happening down there on the port. My dad says the docks attract every crook in the book. So I reckon that's the place to go.

Robbie's dad wasn't going on the expedition. He was feeling rotten. He'd stopped going to work and hadn't been going out lately. Robbie had recovered from the shock of his kidnapping. But it looked as if his dad was still upset about it and, on top of that, all his friends had shunned him since the incident at the hall, cutting him out of their lives.

The car set off at last. Aunt Mari was in front with Robbie's mum, driving slowly in the mist. Unrelenting fields of brown, dripping winter heather, stretched away into the murk, and then the road narrowed and banks of bracken were brushing the sides of the car. The outing was obviously a mistake.

'Here we are!' said Robbie's mum as they approached Gracehill. 'Let's find somewhere to park and we can have a look round.'

The twins and Robbie were packed like sprats in the back of the car, and impatient to get out.

At this hour on a murky February afternoon, most people were tucked up on their sofas watching films or football. Getting everyone together for the outing, with hats, scarves, gloves and binoculars, had taken far too long, and when they finally got there, the few sightseers were already leaving the place; there was a queue of mud-splashed cars pulling out of the miry car park as Robbie's mum drove in.

Aunt Mari told them about the history of the place. The trees had been planted hundreds of years ago to lead up to the new house of Gracehill. James Stuart, who built the house for his wife Grace, thought the trees would make an inviting entrance. But local people had long believed it was more than just an impressive avenue. They believed the trees had powers of their own and warded off evil spirits, protecting the house and village from harm. Some still felt this to be true.

It was bitterly cold and sombre. Brooding clouds were hanging low over the trees. The misty avenue of leafless beeches twined its massive curved arms over the five of them as they walked through. They felt very small and in awe of the monumental dark trees, like a vast intertwined roof of branches above them, as if they were in a sacred place, a cathedral. It was silent; the sound of the departing cars had faded and not a bird sang. It was a chilling place in winter.

Robbie felt as if he was waiting for something, but he didn't know what. There was a sudden flap of wings and a large bird of prey flew along the shadowy tunnel of trunks and branches in front of them – like a spirit guide, thought Robbie. The light was almost too dim to use the binoculars.

The twins, out in front, started racing down the avenue after the bird, which disappeared into the mist. Robbie joined in and the three boys, panting and straining to be the fastest, were soon far in front.

The boys ran towards Gracehill village, and threw themselves down on the damp grass by a big round pond in the village square. When they caught their breath, they stared around.

'What a weird place,' said Charlie. 'It's like living in the old days.'

Among the stone houses there was a large church with a clock tower, flanking one side of the square. They went to investigate. The church door was locked but they followed a narrow path round the back, where they found a damp green churchyard. All the gravestones looked green too, with mould, velvety moss and lichen – and, mysteriously, Robbie thought, every one of the carved slabs was lying flat on the earth.

'I read somewhere that in some countries they spit before leaving the path in a graveyard,' said Harry. 'It wards off evil spirits.'

So they all spat. Then they shared some mints and felt better.

Large trees flanked the green space. Spreading yews with gigantic trunks, and upright pines, broad and tapering, sat in their own forbidding pools of darkness where, it seemed, even darker shadows were flitting.

Churchyards often seem solemn, as if a crowd of the missing is hovering around, unseen but present. It was getting dark as the light withdrew behind the swathe of grey mist. If the sun was going down, it would be impossible to say where; there was no parting glow. It was hard to know what was real.

The three boys, fully alert and not wanting to disturb any invisible spirits, fell silent and walked around the churchyard catlike, inspecting the fallen stones, which seemed like heavy lids designed to keep the dead from rising up. Robbie was sure that if they looked into the darkness, beyond those looming yews and pines, they'd find something real, hiding. He walked quietly towards the trees, but as he stepped into the woods he stood on a twig, snapping it. There was an abrupt clatter of birds' wings that made all three boys jump. They looked at each other and laughed.

At this point the boys heard Aunt Mari calling them from the other side of the church.

'Come on, boys, let's go! We thought we could have tea at Gracehill House. My treat. Come on, or we'll all catch our death out here.'

They were soon sitting down in the large hotel drawing room, a haven of cosy sofas and armchairs, sinking into deep cushions. There was a clatter of teacups and they were cheered by a tray of potato scones with butter, jam and cream. When their plates were empty the waitress showed them a treasure of the hotel, an extraordinary door at the end of the room, which had been carved from the wood of one of the fallen trees from the Dark Hedges.

A tempest, Storm Gertrude, had taken several of these giant trees down in 2016, and a film crew, who were working in the village, rescued the old timber and found someone to carve a whole set of beautiful doors with intricate designs of animals, chains, cups, birds of prey and strange symbols. And bang in the middle of this door was the very bird of prey that Robbie had seen earlier flying away in front of them along the tunnel of trees.

It was now dark outside, and with tea inside them they all felt quite pleasurably scared walking through the fog that had gathered under the trees on the unlit road back to the car park – the Grey Lady, or any other random ghost from the haunted churchyard nearby, might jump out at them at any minute.

Charlie and Harry had picked up sticks and were fighting each other. Robbie found a sturdy stick and ran in to attack. But, concerned about hurting anyone, his way of fighting was to dodge in and out with little thrusts while the twins were really whacking away, wood on wood. The clack-clack of their battle was enough to keep all the ghosts away.

When they got back to Arlen, they dropped Charlie and Harry at their house. Their mother opened the front door to let them in. A cheery shaft of light fell on the road from the doorway and there was a blast of reggae pounding out. The door closed behind them and the light and sound vanished.

They dropped off Aunt Mari and finally drove home to a silent Rappaport Road.

Robbie and his mum sat down to eat a bowl of Heinz

tomato soup. She told him that *Little Shop of Horrors* had been a great success and, on the strength of it, there would be another show. They hadn't decided what it would be yet.

'Will we be in it, Mum? And will the others?' he asked. 'Is Julie going to be there?'

'Yes, I expect so,' she said. 'Would you like to be in it?'

'Yes!' he said. 'It was good fun.'

'Well, you remember that cowgirl singer, SP, the choir leader? As it happens, she's been in touch with me and she wants you take part in whatever they put on next. She says she likes your singing.'

Robbie looked at his mum. Her eyes were shining.

'What about you, Mum?'

'Well, I hope I'll get a part,' she said wistfully. 'Music was such a big part of my childhood – my dad with his accordion, all of us singing. Any chance to sing and we'd sing our hearts out. You haven't had the same, Robbie. It's been a bit of a boring life for you here with me and Dad. I never really thought about it till now. But SP seems to think you have talent and your voice is a bit special.' She leaned over and put her hand on his.

'What would you think about changing schools? We could find a school where they do plays and have lots of music and singing.'

But Robbie was busy forming a plan in his mind and deciding that he needed the twins' help. He realised his mum was waiting for a response so he said, 'Fine.' And thought no more about it.

I'm going to Harry and Charlie's house. I want them to come with me to ask Sandy if he knows of a boat shed that's empty, or maybe even a boat! We could play in it, use it as a hideout. I wonder what happened to that blue boat, the *Blue Fairy*, now those rotten crooks are in prison. Which they deserve.

The twins' mother, Fay, opened the door. Robbie noticed she wore a black scarf with a pattern of white skulls to hold back her straight, fair hair. He thought she looked like a comical pirate. In her hand she had a paintbrush. Her denim overalls were well splashed and she stood dripping green paint on to her gym shoes. She seemed happy to see Robbie. The boys were too. They both held brushes and were helping to paint the kitchen walls green – the green of pistachio ice cream, their mother said.

'Grab a brush, Robbie!' said Fay. Robbie found a spare brush and started to help paint the wall. Bob Marley was playing on the radio again, the reggae producing an energising vibe in the room. While he painted away, Robbie told the twins, under his breath, about his idea...

The next day Robbie and the twins made their way to the fishing quays.

Sandy and Scott were busy, as always, with their nets – and ready, as always, for a chat. The sky was clear and they were gearing up for a long trip out in the North Channel in the *Santa Fay*.

'We're going all out, lads, lots of fish coming in today. Herring shoals or so we heard,' said Scott.

'Mind you, we've had some bad years, all right,' said Sandy, shaking his head. 'Some days the net came up when we were expecting the jackpot – and nothing! Just a few slippery squid covered with black ink or a handful of tiddlers. That's when we went into the lobster pots.'

Scott agreed. 'Those were terrible days, that's when a lot of our mates left the business altogether.'

'I suppose that means there are some empty fishing sheds,' said Robbie craftily, trying to hide his excitement.

'There are plenty of them, all right. There was a time when thirty boats went out from here. Now it's less than a dozen.'

The sheds were behind them, a row of tarred black wooden doors daubed with graffiti. A few were open, radios muttering their litany of shipping forecast areas: 'Lundy, Irish Sea, Rockall, Malin, Hebrides, Bailey, Faeroes, South East Iceland…' In front were piles of fishing nets and gear, together with red, pink and orange floats. But the big, weather-bleached wooden doors were mostly locked. A sudden gust blew dried seaweed and sand along the quay and rocked the boats as they got ready for a night at sea.

'Wind's getting up,' said Sandy. 'We may have it rough later. What's that forecast say, Scott?'

'Good visibility, winds strong to moderate – but I can check with Pete next door. He'll have all the latest.'

Pete's prediction was the same, nothing to worry about, and they started to pile their kit on board.

'Can you swim, Sandy?' said Robbie anxiously. 'I expect you wear life jackets, don't you?'

'I've never learned to swim and I dare say I never will now. But I clip myself to the rail, so I shan't be lost, don't you worry. By the way...' he hesitated before continuing, 'how's that lovely mother of yours?'

'She's OK. She's a bit bored because she doesn't go out enough,' said Robbie, thinking how happy she'd been when they were taking part in the musical. 'She loves dancing.'

'I'd go dancing with her,' said Sandy. 'I like dancing, me.'

The boys soon wandered off, trying to look casually at the sheds without drawing any attention to themselves. They waited until they'd waved the boats off, and then went to work, trying all the locks.

Five minutes later they found what they were looking for – an unlocked boat shed, dry and empty, although it still smelled of fish and oil. There was a tap on the wall, with a sink under it. Harry tried turning on the tap; a gush of water flowed into the sink and straight out on to the floor, where it trickled into a grating, leaving a trail of fish scales glistening on the cement. There were a few pegs on the back of the doors and a light bulb hanging from a beam.

'Where's the switch?' asked Harry.

'I expect the electricity's turned off,' said Robbie.

'This is great, though. This'll do,' said Charlie, excited.

'Let's try it, we can get inside and shut the door.'

The doors were warped, letting in a fair amount of draught.

'We're going to need some warmer clothes,' said Robbie. 'And a torch.'

What the three of them were doing was not *stealing*, Robbie felt, it was only *borrowing* from their parents. They took blankets, plates, mugs, a saucepan and spoons. A backpack was filled with tins of beans and a loaf. They also *borrowed* a camping stove with a small gas cylinder. They *borrowed* a torch. They *borrowed* matches.

That evening, the boys met at Robbie's house. His mum was in the kitchen and she offered them ginger biscuits, which they pocketed, and tea.

'How many sugars?' she said.

Charlie and Harry cried, 'Three, please!' in unison and the kitchen filled with the sound of the boys' laughter.

'Quiet there! Can't you give me some peace, for God's sake?' came an angry voice from the sitting room. Robbie's dad. The three boys looked at each other guiltily.

Robbie's mum was curious to know why they wanted to go out again now it was getting dark. Charlie and Harry both started talking at once.

'We're going to a friend's house to play ping-pong.'

'We're going to help our mum paint the kitchen.'

They looked at each other, laughing again. Robbie quickly intervened.

'We're going to do the painting first,' he said, 'and we'll play ping-pong later. The kitchen's going to be pistachio green,' he added, to give veracity to the story.

'Hmm,' said his mum. Robbie could see she wasn't entirely

convinced, but he knew she'd be glad for Robbie now he had these nice friends and was doing things with them.

'As long as the three of you stay together,' she said, 'and don't get yourselves into any more trouble.'

'We won't,' they said, quickly swallowing the sugary tea and getting their coats. There was a noisy grab for hats and scarves.

'Keep those voices down!' came the voice again from the sitting room.

'Who's seen my torch?'

'Where's my coat?'

'Bye, Mum.'

And they were gone.

Robbie and the twins headed over to Maddy's house. Maddy came to the door herself. She was excited to see the three boys outside. She wanted to hear all about the kidnapping, which had been hushed up, but rumours had been circulating and she'd heard some of the gossip. She invited them in. She called to her mother, who Robbie could see was in their kitchen pouring herself a glass of wine.

'Some friends are here, Mum, I'll take them up to my room.'

'We've got lots to tell you,' said Robbie.

Her eyes were wide as they described their secret new den in the boat shed. But they warned her it was cold in there.

Maddy opened her wardrobe to reveal a whole world of colour and glitter.

'I'm going to be on the stage when I grow up. I want to be in the theatre. Dancing and singing. So most of my clothes won't work for a boat-shed den.'

She started to look through and she brought out a thin glittery cardigan.

Robbie shook his head.

'You need something really warm, haven't you got anything warmer? And you'll need these,' said Robbie, rooting in the bottom of the wardrobe and pulling out a woolly hat and some boots. Maddy found a thick fleecy jumper. A black parka with a cosy fake-fur lining also met with his approval.

They were ready to go.

The children were under the hulls of the large deep-ocean boats, whose looming black prows dwarfed the young crew. The seaweed smell was mixed with the pungent scent of oily fumes. Down here, a denser mist thickened the air and the dim lights had halos. A foghorn called. Waves slopped against the harbour wall, sending wet splatters on to the uneven stone cobbles of the quayside. The dangling bags of their belongings dragged the handlebars of their bikes to one side, making it harder to balance.

'Almost there,' Robbie whispered. The fog was making them short of breath. 'If there's anyone about, let's walk straight past.'

As they arrived, almost panting, at the fishing quay, one last fisherman was setting out, the red and green lights on his boat bobbing. Bent on leaving, he was scarcely aware of the children. He cast off and disappeared with a roar into the drifting vapour. The moored boats creaked and rang their chains.

They stopped in front of the silent, empty shed.

Furtively, they opened it up. Only when they were inside the dim space with the doors shut and their torches on did they feel they could breathe properly again.

They unpacked the blankets and spread them on the hard floor. They lit the little portable stove; the twins had often been camping and they knew how to fix it up, although it was Maddy who warned them they'd have to open a window or the fumes would get them. A can of baked beans was opened and heated in a frying pan. They sat cross-legged round the stove and chatted to each other as they carefully tipped some of the beans into the middle of slices of bread.

'Mmm, this is sooo good,' said Maddy.

'Food always tastes best by a campfire,' said Harry.

'Let's live on beans and never wash again,' said Charlie.

'Right on,' said Robbie. 'Hey, what's for pudding?'

CHAPTER 14

The phone call

Mum and Dad have been arguing. A lot. I usually don't listen, but this time it's about my school. Mum says I should move schools and Dad says no, it will toughen me up to stay where I am. If he asked me, I'd tell him. I'd tell him I hate it. And that I never want to set foot there again. I'd tell him about the noises they make. And how Dodds makes sure no one dares stick up for me. And that he and Victor ran off with my copy of *Treasure Island* that Dad gave me for Christmas and they took it outside and set it on fire. And how stupid Mr Burton said I was clever in front of everyone. It's getting so I daren't speak. I know the answers but I can't say them in case they start again with their noises.

But none of them know about me being a detective. Or about our secret den at the boat shed.

Robbie kept putting things aside to take to the new den. His mother wasn't much of a housekeeper and didn't really notice. She tutted when she realised they'd run out of milk and eggs *again*. And she commented that they seemed to be eating an awful lot of bread these days, and where on earth were those cans of beans she'd only just bought? But it didn't seem to cross her mind that something might be going on.

My dad always reads the local paper on Sunday after church. If they aren't arguing he reads bits out to Mum. Mum has started noticing about the food. At breakfast she said, 'You seem to be eating a lot these days, Robbie, you've eaten the whole packet of Hobnobs.'

I'll have to be more careful. I wonder if Sandy and Scott have noticed us coming and going at the sheds...

Robbie cycled to the quays, having told his mum he was going out to do some birdwatching. There was no one about. But, then, the fishing boats didn't go out on Sundays.

It was a rare day of blue skies and calm sea. Spring was rousing the birds – the seagulls mewed endlessly to each other, playing chase, and he thought it would be nicer to eat lunch outside the shed today. He noticed that the blue kidnap boat, whose cabin was imprinted on his memory, was back on its moorings. It would make a good picnic spot.

He knocked on the door of the shed. The twins and Maddy were already inside.

Robbie suggested his boat picnic idea and everyone agreed. They crossed the quay and climbed on to the blue boat. Robbie opened the bag of provisions and they sat on bench seats at the table in the little cabin. There was a galley and an electric kettle. Robbie thought this was a perfect place for picnics – until another boat, a rather faded navy blue sailboat with an outboard motor, glided slowly towards the quay.

They all bobbed down. Robbie peered as best he could to see what was going on.

On board the boat Robbie could see Aunt Mari, looking almost sporty in jeans and a bright orange life jacket. With her was Brendan Bentham, the boyfriend no one was supposed to know about. He looked comfortable in his faded denim shirt, waterproof trousers and a floppy khaki sun hat, and was quite at ease on the boat. He moored without difficulty and helped Aunt Mari ashore. They were chatting quite openly and Robbie could hear what they were saying.

'I thought I'd have a look round,' said Bentham. 'One of the dock workers mentioned that he's seen your nephew and his gang coming down here with bags of stuff on their bikes.'

'That sounds like Robbie,' said Aunt Mari. 'I expect he's got himself another mystery to solve. What will it be this time, do you think?'

'I don't know,' replied Bentham. 'But I do know that young Robbie has been through a lot recently. He was brave and appears to have come out of it all unscathed. But it won't do any harm to keep an eye on him, check he's all right.'

Bentham started across the quay. 'I think I'll have a look at these empty sheds.'

The children's faces paled. They were all poised ready to fly and Robbie signalled for them to stay down.

Bentham started trying all the doors, pulling them to see if they were locked. When he got to their den the detective pulled the big wooden door wide open. It was heavy and dragging on the cobbles, making a terrible scraping noise as its weight fell on sagging hinges.

'Will you look at this!' Bentham called to Aunt Mari who,

at that moment was turning round, as if she'd felt Robbie's gaze on her.

Robbie ducked down, and Bentham came out of the dark shed, laughing.

'Those kids have made a great little camp for themselves in there. If I didn't know it was only Robbie's gang,' he said, 'I'd think it might have been someone on the run.'

'Hey, anyway, that's definitely Robbie's bike,' said Aunt Mari. Robbie remembered he'd left his bike leaning against the shed.

'Well, he doesn't want to be found.'

The two of them started to stroll back towards their boat.

Robbie tucked himself right down, banging his head on the fire extinguisher under the galley table.

'In you get, hold my hand.'

Robbie heard their boat motoring slowly away, their voices fading as they crossed the calm green water of the harbour. They all waited until the boat was out of sight and breathed a sigh of relief.

Robbie wondered whether Bentham really was concerned about him, or whether he was up to something.

When he got home, his lunch was on the table. Robbie's dad appeared and his voice was harsh.

'You! Just who d'you think you are, keeping us waiting like this! You need to show some respect. We've been waiting here with dinner getting cold for half an hour. I'd be black and blue if I'd ever kept my parents waiting like that, I can tell you that for nothing. You will learn to be punctual, I'll make sure of that.'

There was a dreadful silence. For an instant Robbie's face was a map of injured feelings, which he quickly replaced with a repentant expression. Robbie's mum came rushing in. She was flushed, and gave his dad a look. She seemed cross, but not with Robbie. He could tell she was fed up with his dad.

Robbie bolted the food on his plate and disappeared upstairs.

I asked my dad to come with me to the fishing quays. I want to show him the *Blue Fairy*. It has a notice on saying it's for sale. I thought it would be great to have a boat. Then we can picnic on it without having to hide when someone else comes along. He said he was too busy. So I asked Jeff instead. Jeff's coming to look at it soon; he loves boats.

Robbie was doing a bit of homework at the kitchen table when his dad came storming in. His face was red. He turned viciously on Robbie, pointing to an article in the *Arlen Post*.

'Listen to this, this takes the biscuit. "Local boy Robbie Laggan says he can't wait to audition for the next show at Carrick Hall." You never asked me about this. I will not allow it, not again.'

Robbie saw his mum come into the kitchen, but she didn't intervene. His dad's face was swollen with rage and there was no reasoning with him when he was like this.

'You're nothing but trouble! You would do well to sit here

and read the Gospel of St Luke instead of running around with those boys.'

He turned and looked at Robbie's mum. Robbie wondered if he expected support from her. But she turned and walked out of the room. He turned back to Robbie.

'I know just who to blame for your bad ways. Finding mischief, that's what you're about – and you're learning what? How to disrespect your elders, that's what. Wickedness!'

He held up the newspaper, crumpling it in his hand. Foam flew from his mouth as he shouted, 'The Lord sees it all, the wrath of God will not spare you. There's punishment for youngsters who are out of control. They get what's coming to them!'

Robbie stared at his dad with alarm. His jaw was set, his swollen face flushed purple. When Robbie saw the dark veins pulsing on the side of his dad's forehead and the look in his staring eyes, he jumped up.

'Sorry, Dad,' he said.

He wanted to get away from the house as fast as he could. He'd take his binoculars with him and go to the safety of his camp in the woods. He dashed into the hall, grabbed his binoculars and reached for his coat. His mum stood at the bottom of the stairs, white-faced.

His dad glared at her, his eyes bulging like boiled sweets in their dark sockets.

'You! You spoil the boy,' he spat. 'It's time he had some real discipline and I'm going to see that he gets it.'

'What's he supposed to have done?' asked his mum.

'What's he supposed to have done?' yelled his dad, thrusting the newspaper at his mum. 'Read it for yourself. I'm going out.'

Robbie heard the car door slam. The engine gave a protesting snarl as his dad shot off down the road.

Robbie soon came back from the woods. He couldn't shake a feeling that something was wrong and he wanted to see if his mum was all right. At first, he was quite relieved to find his dad hadn't yet returned, but as the minutes ticked by he could see that his mum was getting more and more anxious.

'I don't know where he's gone,' she said. 'I've never seen your father in such a state.'

They waited, had something to eat, tried watching television. His mum let him stay up to keep her company. By one in the morning, Robbie's mum was pacing anxiously up and down.

The phone rang.

He saw his mum pick it up gingerly, as if it was red-hot. After a few seconds silence, which felt as though it lasted an eternity, Robbie heard his mum speak. He could tell she was scared.

'Surely there's been a mistake, he's always been a very safe driver.'

And Robbie knew. It was the police ... his dad.

They were taken to see him in St Kit's Hospital. He could barely speak. Robbie watched his dad take his mum's hand in his.

He managed to say, 'You're the love of my life, you know.'

His mum smiled at him through tears as he turned his head towards Robbie.

'We're all right, Robbie, aren't we?'

'Yes, Dad,' said Robbie, stepping forward to take his dad's other hand. 'We're fine. Don't worry.'

A monitor started to beep.

A nurse came in to check the drips and take a pulse. She looked at the monitor, which was fluctuating feebly. She turned to Robbie's mum.

'The doctor would like a word with you,' she said, looking grave. She turned to Robbie. 'Will you be all right staying here and keeping your dad company?'

Robbie nodded.

His dad was sleeping. Robbie sat beside him and listened to his insubstantial breathing; there was a silence between each breath which seemed to be getting longer as the minutes passed. He willed the breaths to keep coming, and his mum to come back soon.

But when she did, she was pale and shaky.

'Robbie... I'm afraid your dad's had a heart attack,' she said.

Robbie looked at her, bewildered. He took his dad's hand. It felt normal, warm. He'd recover in time, people did. But when he looked back at his mum, her expression told him it wasn't going to be like that.

They sat together, listening, and looking at his dad's face anxiously for signs that he knew they were there. But there wasn't a flicker. Eventually, the shallow breaths, light as floating thistledown, faded slowly away and the beeping monitor rang out loudly once and started to hum. There were no more breaths. They put their heads together and wept.

It's hard to be at home at the moment. The house is full of people. Everyone has been busy since Dad died. I see them making lists and they say they have to 'make arrangements'. Which means they're always walking off or going out somewhere.

Aunt Mari and Aunt Lizzie are here all the time, and there's always tea on the table, or sometimes other drinks. Boxes of drinks and bottled water have been arriving. There's a huge fruit cake but I've been told not to eat any of it. What's a cake for if you can't eat it?

They don't say anything to me except, 'Are you OK?' Then they kind of look straight through me and go and do something in the kitchen. I can see they're thinking about something else. So I don't say anything. I'm just in the way.

They took me to the funeral place to see Dad. The room smelled of disinfectant or something. When Mum took me in I could see it was him but he looked different. Almost like plastic. I don't want to remember him like that so I didn't look at him for long. But I keep seeing his face. When they took me in to see him I felt he wanted to tell me something. Mum's a bit strange. She says she can't cry these days. It's as if she's not really here. Aunt Mari keeps telling her to sit down and take it easy, but she won't.

After the funeral, people walked to Rappaport Road. They lowered their voices, murmuring, 'Sorry for your loss.' But soon after there were glasses chinking and people were laughing. Robbie's mum was putting out sandwiches and cutting the huge fruit cake into little oblong pieces instead of proper slices. He wondered how they could be happy on such a sad day.

The church had been full for the funeral. Many dockers and ferrymen arrived with their families and every pew was overflowing. The orations were full of praise for a sound man of the Church. The fact that they, his brethren, had cold-shouldered him was never mentioned at all.

Robbie had walked up the aisle, behind what seemed to him like an enormous wardrobe with brass handles, holding his mum's arm. They were followed by all the aunts, uncles and cousins. They came to a stop at the front as the coffin bearers placed the coffin down. Robbie tried to be brave. He couldn't see clearly through the tears on his eyelashes. But beyond the stained glass of the church window he could see a radiant blue sun, bright and strangely consoling. It made him think of heaven. In spite of it all, he'd very much wanted to love his dad and to be loved by him. Touching the wooden side of the coffin with his fingertips he whispered, 'We're all right, Dad, aren't we?'

CHAPTER 15

St Mungo's

Robbie was sitting on the steps that led from the kitchen into the overgrown garden. He was cleaning his hated football boots. He could hear his mum and Aunt Mari chatting and, when he heard his name, stopped rubbing his boots and strained to hear.

'Poor Robbie. You know, I still don't know what I feel about Mark, Mari. I suppose I wish I'd been kinder to him. I know he loved us in his way. But he was always so judgemental, so critical, such a hard, unforgiving father – always on at him about the fear of the Lord. And it made me feel very angry towards him.'

'I think Robbie will be fine, Rose, it just takes time. But it's such a pity he doesn't like his school.'

'I know. Actually, I think it's worse than I'd realised. Did you know two of the boys in his class have it in for him? They make all sorts of noises whenever he tries to answer a question – he told me they're at it again, he said it does his head in.'

'Robbie's not like them. For a boy like him, I never thought that tough school was the right choice at all, Rose. Did you?'

'Well, it wasn't my choice. I definitely want to find him a better school for next September. Maybe I can find out more about St Mungo's where the twins go to school. Then we'll go and see what it's like.'

Robbie decided he should join this conversation, but as soon as he came indoors, they started talking about something else.

I went to see the twins and they talked to me about my dad, which is more than most of the adults I know have managed to do. They said it was OK without a dad, and their mum is on her own too. I asked Fay if she was lonely. She laughed and said she was very lonely, but she's looking for someone to go out with. I think my mum would like someone to go out with too.

Fay gave me a cupcake with green icing and silver balls on it. I think she likes green. She said how very sorry she was about Dad.

She told me there's going to be a talent contest in the summer and we can all go in for it. Mum hasn't said much about it. But Fay says I should enter, and that the forms will be up in the arts centre. She said she really thought I had a good chance. So I'm going to have a go.

I played ping-pong with the twins. I'm not that good at it, but I won twice.

After that we went down to the fishing quays to see Sandy and Scott. I like Sandy. He was singing and he can play the guitar. He said he sometimes plays and sings at the Ifflick Bar. So I think he would make a good boyfriend for Mum.

It would be cool if he entered the talent contest. I think I'll get him a form. I asked him for his whole name and he said it was Alexander Sitwell.

Spring came and went with a rushing and gushing of gutters and drains. Robbie had talked to his mum about the talent contest and she gave him her blessing. She found him a song he liked and he was practising singing it as he pedalled up the hill to the arts centre.

By the time he got there he was out of breath. He threw himself down in a patch of sunlight on the unkempt lawn in front of the building; it was full of blue speedwell and yellow dandelions. The upstairs windows were open and there were bees about.

From the corner of his eye he saw a small blue-and-yellow bird fly past his head at speed and bang into a window. It fell to the ground, stunned. He ran over and picked it up; it was warm and so light in his hand.

He took it inside and looked for Julie. She was there in bright yellow dungarees, reminding Robbie of a buttercup.

They inspected the bird. It started to struggle feebly in his hand and pecked his finger with all its tiny might. Startled, Robbie let it go and it started fluttering round the office. They tried to catch it, jumping around and climbing on the desk, sending papers flying everywhere. Eventually, they thought of opening the window and it flew out to safety.

Robbie helped pick up the papers from the floor. Among the scattered papers he spotted some forms for the talent contest.

'Can I have some of these?' he asked.

'They're like gold dust, those forms. We've had to limit the number given out or the contest would be unmanageable. We hadn't anticipated the high demand,' said Julie.

'Oh please, Julie..'

'Well, I suppose you can have a few. What will you do with them?'

'I've got some people who want to go in for it,' said Robbie. 'I'll take them round.'

'Well, do it soon,' said Julie, 'otherwise they might miss the boat.'

'OK, thanks!' he said, disappearing rapidly out of the door with a good handful of forms before she had a chance to protest.

I know quite a lot of people who could be in the talent contest. I never used to know all these people who like the same things as me. Most of the boys at school only like football. I'd like to join in but I don't like games because Dodds and Victor always make a point of running straight at me and trying to knock me over. It's not just that it hurts – it makes me feel they're out to get me, like hunting an animal. I wonder what a rabbit feels like when it's hunted. I remember reading about Brer Rabbit and how clever he was; he was always one up on the fox. I should find a way of being one up on Dodds.

Before, I always thought there was something wrong with me because I'm not good at sport. Dad always wanted me to get into the football team and do cricket and boxing. But now I can see that different people are good at different things. Maybe if I try hard at the singing, I can show him what I'm good at. I hope he'll be pleased ... if he can hear me.

I'm also going to do some more detective work. Sandy told me that Jeff and Windy have been seen together in the Ifflick Bar again. He said people had started to see Jeff in a different light recently – not, as my dad thought, a lazy skiver, but a man with a job that he loves – a police diver! But what is he doing with Windy Wake, the dancer? Why are Jeff and Windy friends?

Everyone has secrets. Mum has secrets. I remember seeing her getting the parcel with the red dress like a huge flower. She wore it to go dancing. Maybe she can wear it for the talent contest. I think Mum is longing to sing and go dancing again. She loves music and so does Sandy. I wonder if he has any secrets. Jeff was really secretive about joining the Dive Unit. And Aunt Mari has secrets too – why doesn't she want to tell anyone about her seeing DI Bentham?

It must be all right if you don't tell everything, it's normal.

It isn't the same as lying. Is it?

Robbie was having lunch with the twins. He thought the lunch tasted especially good, but wasn't sure what they were eating.

'It's parmigiana di melanzane,' said Fay. 'It's Italian – aubergines.'

'I've never had aubergines before.' I don't really know what they are.'

'You'll have to go to Italy one day,' she said. 'They eat a lot of them there.'

'Yes,' said Robbie, 'I'd like to go there. Someone told me it's the Land of Song.'

'Then you must go to Venice where there are no cars, only boats, and they have an opera house and the boatmen all go around in straw hats, singing songs in Italian.'

'Yes! That sounds awesome,' he said. 'I'd like that, can we all go?'

'Maybe we should,' said Fay.

When his mum came to pick him up Fay invited her in. They started to chat.

Entering detective mode once more, Robbie did a good job of appearing not to be listening as his mum said, 'So do the boys like their school? Robbie hates his. His father chose it. It's quite tough and it's boys only.'

'That sounds a bit rubbish. Well, yes, they do rather like it,' said Fay. 'It's inclusive and welcoming, and there are girls there. I love it because they're very keen on encouraging the children. Maddy goes there, and you know she wants to be a singer. And Robbie is so musical. It's quite arty and creative and the music is really good.'

'It sounds as if it might really suit him,' said Rose. 'He's putting a brave face on things, but he's missing his dad and needs a bit of encouragement, and he could certainly do without being bullied. There are some nasty bullies in his year.'

'He must dread going in. Lucky he always seems to have lots going on in his life.'

'Yes, he does like to get involved in all sorts of things,' said Rose.

We've come to see the twins' school, St Mungo's, and I think I like it. Maddy is showing us round. It isn't as big as my school. There are gardens outside and I can hear people practising the piano and guitar together in the music rooms. It's a good idea to have special rooms for music. There are rooms for people to do industrial design and painting and make pots. They have drama classes and singing, which Maddy likes, and there's a proper stage in the hall. Everyone wears what they want, but I don't really know what I want to wear.

It's hard because you have an interview and take an exam to get in. I could try, but I'd be scared of failing the exam.

Maybe I should stay put for now. Dad wanted me to go to my school. He said it would toughen me up, that I should stand up to bullies. He thought not fitting in was a bad sign, that it was better to just say it was all OK and act like I was the same as they were.

But I can't be the same as the bullies. I don't want to be like that. They bully younger boys as well. I don't like it and I can't do it just to be one of them. So I don't have friends there. Everyone laughs at me and Dodds and Victor are out to get me. Here I'd have the twins and Maddy, who aren't like that. I'd better ask Aunt Mari if she thinks I could pass the exam. I think I'll give it a go.

On the day of the exam Robbie woke up with an unusual feeling in his stomach that was half excitement and half terror. When they got there, the school – a rambling old country house in a park – was tranquil, the children still away for half-term. It was Robbie's turn for the interview with the head teacher. He was shown into a comfortable room with faded flowered curtains and sagging sofas.

As she sat smiling, with a comfortable air about her, the head did not look like head of anything. She spied Robbie and gave a delighted cry.

'Welcome to St Mungo's! I'm the head teacher. We use first names here, so call me Sue. I heard you gave a great performance in the show at the Carrick Hall recently. You'll love all the music and drama here. How have we managed without you all this time? Come and sit down and tell me all about it.'

She listened to Robbie telling the story of auditioning for the show and how much fun it'd been.

'Now, Mrs Laggan, why don't Robbie and I get to know each other while you go and have a look around?'

She turned to Robbie again and started a conversation with him about singing. He began to relax.

CHAPTER 16

Out of the frying pan

Robbie, with trepidation, was getting ready to play football. He went to his locker to get his kit. He opened the door and stepped back sharply – from inside came a putrid smell and he found something foul, which turned out to be a rotting grey squirrel, in one of his boots. In the other was a scrunched up piece of paper. He unfolded it and read the words: 'We will get you.'

He looked round the locker room to see if there was someone watching him. Someone who wanted to see him jump. There was nobody from his class in sight, but he knew well enough who'd done this: Dodds and Victor – the worst things in Robbie's life. He was incensed by the sight of the dead animal. A cruel, senseless act. He'd had enough.

I'd better get off football today. I don't want to be kicked to bits. I wouldn't put it past them to knock my teeth out on the pitch and say it was an accident. I can say I feel sick – it's true, I do feel sick. That poor squirrel. What a stink. How could they?

While they're playing, I'm going to look in their lockers. It's fair enough; they've been in mine.

If Dodds and Victor want a war they can have one. I'm

going to watch them and find out their horrid secrets. It's hard to do it on my own, but they'll see – I'm not such a wimp as they think I am. They think that being bullies will get them on top. But it's better to be able to use your brains. I'm a detective and I'll get the goods on them. If I think about it, I do have a trick or two up my sleeve, and I'm making a plan. They're heading for a fall. They'll see.

Robbie reported in sick and disposed of the squirrel. The note he kept.

He sat on a bench to get it all straight in his mind. It was *necessary* to look in their lockers, but was it *wrong*?

His father's voice was speaking to him. 'It's tit for tat, boy. But you mustn't take anything out. That would be stealing.'

In this way he settled his conscience and went to look in the lockers. He found a good deal that he'd rather not have found. Things that must belong to other boys, like watches. And his bicycle chain – he was pretty sure it was his. And a knife! In Dodds' locker! Finally, he unfolded a piece of paper to find a drawing of a person with a chain round his neck. Underneath it said 'RL'. His initials!

At this moment, there was a click. Robbie cocked his ears. Someone had opened the locker room door and was heading this way. He put the drawing back in, shut the locker door as quietly as he could and turned round. Mr Burton, looking decidedly unsteady, was glaring at him, beer bottle in hand, as he approached.

'What's all this now, what's this?' he said in a thick voice.

'What shenanigans are you up to, Laggan? Are you not on the football field at this time of the day?'

'I'm not well, sir,' said Robbie. 'Mr Roddy said I could skip football today.'

'Well, you can't stay in here. Get along to the sick bay and tell Miss Cawfield.' It seemed to Robbie that he swayed slightly as he spoke. 'Or go on home, what do I care? Go on! Chop-chop!'

Robbie had left the things in the lockers undisturbed. He didn't want the two bullies to know he was on to them. His first thought was to set a trap for them. He thought of luring them to the boat shed and locking them in. But then what? They had to be seen for what they were: thugs. But he was worried about the bicycle chain and the drawing – they had a plan to attack him, he was sure.

He cycled up to see Julie. She was on reception at the arts centre and took him into the room at the back. Her pink hair was in little corkscrew curls today, and her pale face was adorned with glitter round her eyes. She was a beacon of colour in Robbie's otherwise grey day.

She found a packet of florentines and asked Robbie if he wanted tea. When she'd poured him a mug she said, casually, 'I heard from your mum that you don't like your school much, and maybe you're going to St Mungo's? The twins will be pleased.'

Robbie felt comfortable with Julie. He decided to talk to her.

'There are lots of things I don't like about it,' he said. 'The teachers are boring, there's no drama, only the choir is

OK. And there are some bigger boys in my class who want to get me.'

'Do they really?' said Julie. 'Why would they want to do that?'

'They call me a wimp,' he said. 'They're always trying to wind me up by making noises when I speak in class. And they try to threaten me. But now it's got worse.'

'Why, what's happened?'

'Today they put a dead squirrel in my locker and a note saying they were coming for me.'

'That's well scary,' said Julie.

'Yes, and then I went and looked in *their* lockers, and they had a knife and a bicycle chain, and a picture of a person with a chain round their neck and my initials underneath.'

Robbie sounded close to tears.

'Oh, I see. God! Is that why you're not at school? I thought it wasn't your style to bunk off.'

'I was afraid if I played football they might kick my head in, so I said I was sick.'

'Well, I can see you need to get them off your back somehow.'

'What do you think I should do?' he said, nibbling a florentine and feeling the nuts getting stuck in his braces.

'Robbie, be careful. Whatever you do, don't ever let them find you alone. Seriously! It sounds like they've got it in for you, and they could be dangerous.'

'They're getting scary, so I try to avoid them anyway.'

'Good,' said Julie. 'And by the way, you're great, don't let them make you feel bad. They're jealous of you because you're cleverer than them. Just go on being you, Robbie, and you'll find a way of dealing with it, I'm sure of that. And by the way, Rafferty and I both think you're in with a chance at the talent contest.'

Robbie felt a bit better. 'Thanks, Julie,' he said.

As he cycled home to Rappaport Road he kept turning to look over his shoulder, to see if anyone was following him. Not this time. But now he thought about it, a detective should be *doing* the following, not being followed.

On Friday, Robbie's mum had an appointment after school with the head of Saint Mungo's and wanted Robbie to go with her to hear whether he'd got a place. He got through the day at school without being on his own once and managed to get home all right.

There were floating columns of gnats rising and falling over the lawn as they walked up to the school entrance. Robbie's mum was wearing her new flowered dress. The evening was warm and the silk looked cool and floaty. He noticed a little label dangling from the top of the zip at the back of her neck, but they didn't have time to sort it out so he decided not to say anything.

They rang the bell.

'Well now, don't you look lovely, the pair of you,' said the head teacher as she welcomed them in. She noticed the dangling label and said, 'Shall I take this off for you?' in a motherly way. Robbie looked at his mum and she was smiling and seemed relaxed as the label was removed. Robbie felt he was in safe hands.

'Well, it's all good news. We've found a place for Robbie and he can start in September.' Robbie's heart leaped. No more bullying. No more boring, and even occasionally drunk teachers! Robbie was so excited. He turned to his mum and hugged her.

'As you know,' continued Sue, 'there are grants available for pupils transferring from state schools. You, Robbie, will receive one and another is going to Billy Dodds. He's in your class, I believe, Robbie, so that'll be good news for you.'

Robbie's blood stopped in his veins. Dodds would still be there, threatening him, forever breathing down his neck, out to get him. Unless he could get him off his back. He must find a way.

CHAPTER 17

Know your enemy

It was hot. The day started with a blue haze over the meadows behind Robbie's house, a mist that soon burned off. It seemed so lucky that this fine weather had started on a Saturday. He and the twins were going to take a picnic and go to the beach. He found his trunks and a towel and made himself a peanut butter sandwich. He took a bottle of red lemonade out of the fridge and went to say goodbye to his mum, who was lying in bed with a bad dose of laryngitis.

She'd said she felt so unwell she couldn't face going anywhere and that she was relieved Fay wanted to take Robbie off swimming.

'Fay's going to take you in the car,' she'd said, in a whisper. 'And whatever you do, don't go out of your depth, Robbie, stay in the shallow water. Promise?'

'Yes, Mum, I know.'

'And say thank you, and have fun.'

At Fay's house there was pandemonium. Shouts of 'Where's the sun cream?' and 'That's too small, I can't wear that!' and 'What did you do with my goggles?' rang through the house.

Somehow, between helping them find things and collecting rugs and sun hats, Fay managed to make a packed lunch and put it in the boot of her car.

'How's your mum?' she said to Robbie as they piled into the car.

'Coughing,' he said. 'And she's still a bit croaky at the moment. She can't talk, and she's staying in bed because she wants to get better before the finals of the talent contest.'

'Well, you three boys made it through. Isn't that wonderful?' said Fay as she started the car. 'You're all in with a chance. Now, I thought we'd try Brown's Bay. It's not windy today, should be calm. I bet it's cold in the sea, though – who's going to be first in?'

'You!' said the twins in unison.

'Not a hope in Hades,' said Fay.

The car was hot and by the time they got there they really did want to get into the sea. It was calm, and transparent waves rippled temptingly over the sand. Fay set up the picnic on the grassy dune above the beach, in a hollow sheltered by gorse bushes. Robbie scanned the beach with excitement and took a deep breath of sea air. The gorse smelled of coconut, tiny birds were twittering and everything sang of the coming summer. The boys changed and rushed down to the water.

As Robbie ran he could see from the corner of his eye that two boys were playing footie in the distance. He could hear the hollow thumps as the ball flew in the air.

They plunged into the sea up to their waists, giving themselves a shock of cold as they ducked in up to their armpits and then jumped up out again. The water was glacial.

The two distant boys advanced along the beach. They

had an old leather football that spun in the air as they kicked it to each other.

When they reached Robbie and the twins, they stopped and turned towards them. One of the boys kicked the ball at Robbie. Just as Robbie recognised Dodds and Victor, he managed to dive sideways, and the ball hit the sea with a splash. Robbie emerged coughing. Charlie rescued the ball and threw it back before Robbie had chance to tell him who the boys were. Dodds caught the ball, now heavy with seawater, and ran nearer. He aimed and threw as hard as he could. It hit Robbie squarely on the chest knocking the wind out of him. He fell back into the sea again.

When he came up, Robbie was bent over gasping and winded, a big pink mark glowing painfully on his ribs. Charlie and Harry swam over to him looking concerned. Robbie told them who they were.

The twins glared indignantly at Dodds and Victor. Charlie threw the football as far as he could out to sea, the waves picking it up surprisingly quickly.

Dodds started shouting, 'You can't do that, you idiot! You get that ball back here!'

'Go get it yourself,' said Charlie.

'That's his dad's, that ball, it's his,' said Dodds, pointing at Victor. 'He'll have your guts.'

'Too bad,' said Charlie, squaring his shoulders and stepping closer to Dodds. Harry came up behind his brother.

Dodds and Victor backed off and stayed helplessly on

the beach as they watched the ball floating further and further out to sea. Then they wandered off.

The twins and Robbie walked back to Fay and unpacked their lunch. Robbie, now recovered, ate his squashed-up sandwich, and then Fay shared their picnic with him. After some cold roast chicken he felt much better. Fay asked him exactly what had happened.

'I saw it from up here,' she said. 'I was just about to come down when the boys backed off.'

'They're at my school,' said Robbie, 'in my class. They don't like me very much.'

'It looked as if they were throwing that football at you deliberately,' said Fay.

'They were, Mum!' said Harry. 'They were trying to hit Robbie. You should have felt it, that old football, it was wet and you've no idea how heavy it was.'

'Well, I'm glad you're changing schools, Robbie, you don't need people like that around you!'

'But that's what's so unfair,' he said. 'The big one, Dodds, is coming to St Mungo's with me!'

'Well, they'll soon sort him out there,' said Fay, handing out the beach towels. 'They don't stand for bullying there at all.'

But Robbie didn't feel so confident about that. He had to find a way to stand up for himself.

Charlie and Harry saw that pig Dodds when we went to the beach and they saw what he's like. And his sidekick

Victor, too. They were out to spoil our swimming. In fact, I think they'd have been glad to see me drown.

Harry says it's not fair for the two of them to gang up on me like that. But I think it's really Dodds who wants to get me. Victor just follows his lead in everything. My dad always said I should stand up for myself. He'd be pleased if I can see them off.

I suppose I might need help, but I know I can do it. First of all I have to watch them, watch their movements. See where they go and that sort of thing. I'll keep a notebook. I'm going to find out all about them.

Robbie was in the classroom. Dodds and Victor weren't around and the other boys were lounging about between lessons – yawning, cracking jokes and chatting.

Robbie wasted no time in starting his research. He started by asking around. Billy Dodds, as it turned out, was not much liked. The boys thought him annoying. His so-called teasing ways often got them into trouble. But it seemed he could manipulate them into doing things that sometimes went against the grain.

'He likes getting everyone in a huddle,' they said. 'And he comes up with some joke to play on his latest victim; he's got it in for you, Robbie.'

Robbie knew that for Dodds, tormenting people was fun, even more so if he could get everyone else at it too. If the others ever resisted, he would start shoving them; pushing was followed by jabbing little punches. He would go on sniggering and pretending it was a game. The little punches would get bigger and nastier, so at this point most boys, for the sake of peace, would give up and agree to join in.

There was more.

One boy, Chris O' Dowd, lived in the same street as Dodds. Although Chris had never actually stuck up for Robbie, he'd never joined in either, not like the others. Robbie found he enjoyed chatting to him. Chris knew the whole Dodds family and Robbie was interested to find out that Billy Dodds had no dad. Just his mother, his older brother and his two tiny sisters. His mother had a reputation for selling dodgy stuff; she was well known to the police. You could get whatever you needed from her: mixers, hairdryers, vacuum cleaners, game consoles, sports kit, footballs – even wild animals, snakes and things, it was rumoured. Billy's older brother Jess, at the tender age of fifteen, was already a real hard case and away at a special boarding school.

I always thought everyone liked Dodds. I remember when I got braces on my teeth, I went into school and Dodds started pointing and sniggering at me. At break he got everyone in the class together and they were giggling and whispering. I thought they were all muckers. They carried on until Mr Burton came in and then they shut up. It was horrible. They always end up doing what Dodds wants.

Mostly I keep quiet and don't talk to any of them.

But now I'm doing my research and asking them things, they don't seem all that bad and they think Dodds is awful.

They said Dodds doesn't have a dad.

Like me.

I miss my dad. He was always there, my dad. Now he's not there, it's not the same. But I wonder if he can still see me.

I want him to see me singing at the talent contest.

Mum will be there, and Julie and my friends. And Sandy.

CHAPTER 18

'A dog starv'd at his master's gate, predicts the ruin of the state'

I've been learning a few things about Dodds and now I'm going to start following him. I'm staking him out. I think it's better if I go on my own. If I take the twins he'll see us right away. Maybe Chris O'Dowd can take me to his house; he lives on the same street as Dodds. I can watch his house and see what goes on. Then I can make a plan. I've got him in my sights now. I think my dad would be glad about that.

I'll take my binoculars. It's called surveillance.

You have to wait around a lot. And you mustn't be observed by the suspect.

You build a profile of them. It's important to know where he lives and what his weak points are. After that, I'll know how to hit back. I could sabotage his bike, like he did with mine. I have a special tool for my bike. I can put that in my pocket so I can prise his chain off. Then he'll be late for school and get an earful from Mr Burton. That would be a start.

Robbie, not at all sure what the answer would be, asked Chris

O'Dowd if he could go along with him after school so he could see where Dodds lived.

'OK, if you want to,' he said.

They got on their bikes and rode together to a part of town that was normally out of bounds to Robbie.

The grey streets were coloured with lavish murals, like in the more turbulent areas of Belfast. Robbie saw tower blocks rising up above shuttered shops with barred windows. It was on the border of the Catholic area and disputes went on daily. Every week the police were called to some incident or other.

Chris lived in a neat terrace house right on the street. He pointed out where Dodds lived, over the road. It was at the end of a row and next to it was a yard. He opened his front door with a key and signalled for Robbie to bring his bike inside.

'Shush,' he said. 'Me ma is sleeping. We've got a baby.'

Chris told Robbie his stepfather, Kevin, who was always complaining and found kids annoying, had moved out to live with his gran. The baby upstairs was his, but he hadn't liked being woken up at night. Chris was glad he'd gone.

It seemed to Robbie that nobody had a dad.

They went into the front room and had a look out at the Dodds' house from behind the curtains. It looked unkempt and empty.

'Does it have a garden behind?' asked Robbie.

'Not likely!' said Chris. 'There's just that scruffy old yard over there on the side, see, with a privy?'

A baby started crying upstairs, making a weak sound like a mewing cat.

'I'll make some tea,' he said. 'I'll take a mug up to Mam.'

Robbie sipped his tea while Chris was upstairs and, when he came back down, Robbie decided to take him into his confidence.

'If I tell you something, you won't tell Dodds, will you?'

'Cross my heart and fry my brains in batter,' he said.

'I'm fed up with Dodds and Victor having a go at me,' Robbie said, 'and I'm going to get even.'

'In your dreams!' said Chris. 'Let's see now, how're yer going to do it?'

'I don't know yet. I'm going to see what goes on and make a plan.'

'Sure, well, good luck to you. They're a bad lot.' Chris glanced across the road for a moment. 'That house is full of strange goings-on – noises, things moving around, shadows like, and sometimes at night I see things, animals, from my bedroom window. There's always something lurking in their yard.'

The boys went out, crossed the street and crept round the side of the yard, Robbie looking out for Dodds' bicycle.

When he asked Chris about it, he laughed and said no bikes were left on the street around here because as soon as you weren't looking, it was stolen or the wheels were taken off. A car, subsiding in the gutter with no tyres, proved his point. They thought it would provide good cover and squatted behind it. They could see the top of a wooden shack.

Chris tugged at Robbie's sleeve.

He whispered, 'Let's take a look over the fence.'

Glad of Chris's company, Robbie started to creep forwards, alert and buzzing with curiosity.

They sneaked out from behind the car and across the pavement. The fence was too high. Chris was taller than Robbie and very strong; he gave Robbie a leg up. His head topped the fence and he clung on with both elbows.

The yard was dingy and filthy. By the wall, he saw heaps of what looked like boxes, stacked up under tarpaulins. From behind the boxes a pale, lanky creature loomed into view, a mournful sight, mangy and bony with transparent skin and ribs like a grill pan. Head down, it was sniffing about and shivering. When it saw Robbie it gave a doleful whimper which ended as a yawn, and wandered over to the old wooden privy. Robbie tumbled back on to the pavement.

'You really did see something!' he whispered to Chris. 'There's something living there all right. I think it's a greyhound.'

They stole away back to Chris's house.

I'm thinking about what to do next. Maybe I could hold that poor dog to ransom.

Those men on the *Blue Fairy* were clever. They tricked me and made me their hostage. Then they could ask Dad to do whatever they wanted.

That dog I saw at the Dodds' house needs to get out of there. I could rescue it and make it into a hostage. My conditions would be:

Number 1: I will not give it back until Dodds leaves me alone.

Number 2: They have to look after the dog properly.

Number 3: Dodds gives back my bicycle chain.

But where can I put the dog? It's quite big. Maybe I can keep it at home in my bedroom. I wonder if Mum would notice?

By the next day Robbie had a plan. With a bit of magical thinking he had turned his dognapping idea into a rescue mission. He hoped that if he brought the dog home and pleaded with her, his mum would agree to look after a 'rescue' dog. Just for a few days, or a week or two, while the owners couldn't take care of it themselves. He was itching to get going.

He'd noticed there was a padlock and chain on the gate of the Dodds' yard. He got on his bike and pedalled as fast as he could to the quay. The *Santa Fay* was moored up. He threw his bike down. Noises were coming from on board. He called out.

'Sandy, hey, it's me, Robbie!'

Sandy's head emerged from the hold.

'Hello, Robbie! You're all out of breath. What's the problem?'

Robbie hadn't been sure whether to confide in Sandy, but decided he trusted him.

'Please can I borrow a pair of cutters to cut a chain?'

'What's that for then?' said Sandy, looking up at Robbie and smiling.

'You swear you won't let on if I tell you? Not anyone?' said Robbie.

'Oh, go on then, I promise,' said Sandy.

'I'm going to rescue a starved dog tonight,' said Robbie. 'I'm hoping Mum will look after it for a few days.'

'Your mum can't do that. Hasn't she got a new job at the arts centre? Helping them organise that talent contest? And you'll be at school.'

'But the poor thing is shut up in a filthy yard with no food and it's awfully thin. It's a greyhound.'

'So you think you might be doing them a favour, taking away a dog they don't want to look after?' Sandy winked at Robbie.

'I promise, it's deadly serious!' said Robbie. 'If it stays there in that awful place, it'll starve to death.'

It was settled. Sandy would look after the greyhound; he lived on his own and could do what he liked. But the hard bit was still to come.

CHAPTER 19

Dawn raid

The pearly moon was already dimming in the clear sky. Robbie had got up before dawn. He was walking in the grey light, through unfamiliar and deserted streets. The houses were dark and the gulls were sleeping on the rooftops. He'd dressed quietly and crept out of the house. The hood of his jacket was up and he had with him a pair of metal cutters, pieces of ham and a thin rope. He was on a mission.

The first stumbling block was finding the place. He couldn't exactly remember, and everything looked different now he was on his own and on foot. He walked and walked through the district Chris had brought him to. They'd got there so easily and quickly yesterday. As the day gradually broke, the light made it easier to recognise the streets and he finally arrived at Chris's street just as one or two early risers were starting to stir. But the Dodds house was still and the curtains, if you could call them that, were closed to the cool morning.

He went round the side of the house to the yard gate. He struggled to cut the chain. It was too strong. He attacked it again and again, getting increasingly red in the face and furious. He jumped when he heard a door closing and turned quickly. A figure was standing outside Chris's house. As it walked towards him, Robbie recognised the figure as

Chris. He let out a breath he hadn't known he was holding.

Chris said he'd been up with his baby sister, to give his ma a bit of sleep. He had the baby with him. He'd seen Robbie from his window and guessed who it was. He handed Robbie the baby, a warm, woolly bundle smelling of yoghurt. He took the cutters and with one snap the chain was off.

Clutching the baby, Robbie watched Chris stealthily open the gate. He turned to Robbie.

'Man!' he said. 'What the hell's in those crates?'

They crept forwards. Robbie handed the baby back and lifted a corner of the tarpaulin covering the stacks of crates.

Underneath were rows of cages. Cowering in the back of the first one were several ferrets who, twitching their whiskers, stared at him with red eyes. Huddled in the depths of another was a scruffy chihuahua and underneath that was a skeletal Siamese cat, its blue eyes sticky and half closed.

'You better hurry. Where's this greyhound then?' whispered Chris. They stole across the yard, the ground thick with muck and stinking sawdust, to the privy and opened the door wide. The grey dawn light showed a flat white shape in the gloom.

Robbie got the rope and the ham out of his pocket. 'Here boy,' he whispered. The greyhound, lying flat on its side, slowly raised its head. It stretched, struggled to its feet and came slowly over, dragging a chain which was fastened to a hook on the wall.

Robbie offered the ham and the dog gulped it down. Unchaining the animal, he tied the rope gently round its neck and started to coax it out of the shed with more ham. It followed him across the yard and into the street.

Chris said, 'Good luck, mate,' and gave him a thumbs up. With the baby cradled cosily on his chest, he went back to his house and disappeared quietly inside.

Robbie set out across town with the bag of bones on its rope trotting beside him, its head down low between its sharp shoulders as it left what had been home without a backward glance.

The small hooded boy and the large dog walked on through the dawn, in streets that were nearly deserted.

The occasional motorbike passed. He saw a group of women with buckets and long mops going to their early-morning cleaning jobs, and a taxi heading in the direction of the airport. Robbie, who had kept his head well down, now looked up at the sky, milky white in the early morning. He decided on a name for the dog. He would call him Skywalker. Sky for short. He wondered how he could help the other neglected animals he'd seen in the yard.

It was almost six when Robbie finally arrived at the quay with his rescue dog plodding along behind him, barely able to lift one paw in front of the other. Sandy was in the hold of the *Santa Fay* making a pot of coffee but came straight out when he heard Robbie call to him.

Sandy jumped on to the quay.

'Love the dog,' he said, 'but I must get you home before your mother sees you're gone and starts thinking you've been kidnapped again. I've been wondering what on earth

I'd say to her if you'd gone and got yourself into trouble.'

He took the cutters and the greyhound from Robbie, gave the animal a reassuring pat on the head and shut it in his boat shed with a bowl of water and some dog biscuits he'd bought. Robbie was pretty sure he noticed a nice warm blanket in there too before the doors closed. Maybe Sandy was more of a dog lover than he'd known.

Robbie was exhausted, but on the short drive his excitement bubbled up and he started to fill in Sandy with some of the highlights of the mission.

'It felt like I was lost for hours. And I couldn't cut the chain, but Chris managed it in the end while I held the baby.'

'What?' said Sandy. 'Whose baby was that?'

'Chris was looking after it for his ma. He lives over the road. He's all right, Chris, he's in my class. He came over to help.'

'OK, well, that's good.'

Sandy pulled up outside their house. Robbie had just managed to get into bed and fall asleep when his mum came into his bedroom and woke him up.

'It's time to get up,' she said. 'Why are you sleeping in your outdoor clothes?'

Robbie soon heard the gossip. The Dodds had lost their dog and a small hooded figure with a limping greyhound had not gone unnoticed by a group of early-morning cleaners who'd passed by on their way to work. The chain had been cut on the Dodds' gate and soon the whole district was alive with speculation. But nobody knew who the dognapper was.

Robbie learned that it was well known Mrs Dodds neglected her animals, so there was little sympathy for the family, and she, for obvious reasons, refused to report the theft.

The police, however, had found out about the crime. Robbie's Aunt Mari told him what had happened because Brendan Bentham had got wind of it and thought the police should crack down hard on animal cruelty. Rebecca John of the *Arlen Post* had rung police headquarters and asked if they'd apprehended the greyhound's abductor. On her information – from one of her sources, she'd said – a valuable racing greyhound, many times a winner, had been stolen. Two officers turned up at the Dodds' house to get more details on the crime.

When they saw the filthy yard, they realised the real crime might be closer to home. What they found in the small, dirty cages was enough to make even a hardened officer struggle to hide his disgust. There were the starving ferrets and a litter of hungry kits, some yellow snakes, a cage of moulting chinchillas and the poor Siamese cat.

Worst of all was a frail ghost of a monkey, cramped up and shivering, looking at them with pleading golden eyes.

Inside the house, which smelled of rotting fruit, they'd found a hoard of cardboard boxes full of hairdryers, power washers, vacuum cleaners and other electrical stuff. They asked Mrs Dodds to come down to the station.

'It's me son,' she'd said, 'it's his fault.' She'd tried to smile, to appeal to them as they pushed her into the police car. 'Me son, he's supposed to feed them, and he collects stuff,' she'd protested.

Without evidence that it *was* the sly and crafty Mrs Dodds and not her son, they'd had to release her. But Bentham organised the rehoming of all the animals and put her under surveillance. He discovered that she was something of a powerhouse, a very busy entrepreneur. Her business in stolen electrical goods was only a sideline. When the police searched her house again, they found packing cases and cages full of snakes and four-legged reptiles of all kinds, including baby alligators, rare iguanas and valuable tortoises, all kept in cramped spaces, some inside the kitchen cupboards. All were living in the most slovenly conditions. Rent was paid on a lock-up garage up the road. More horrors were revealed there.

At school the next day Robbie felt like a sleepwalker, but when he saw Chris he felt better. Chris gave him a thumbs up and winked at him as he slid into his seat. Robbie tried to wink back, but was keeping his eye on the door, hoping Mr Burton would arrive quickly in case Dodds saw Robbie's state and made a connection.

'Are you worried, Dodds?' said Chris. Robbie froze but didn't dare turn to look at Dodds.

'Worried? Me? No, why should I be?' said Dodds.

'Oh, no reason,' said Chris. 'Just wondering.' And he started to hum, 'How Much Is That Doggie in the Window?'

'How's yer dog?' said Chris, a minute later. He couldn't keep the secret. He was bursting with it.

'What dog?' said Dodds, setting his jaw.

'Yer greyhound. How's yer prize-winning greyhound?'

Chris was out to cause trouble.

Dodds spat out, 'None of yer damn business,' and started towards Chris, who jumped up and came out into the narrow space dividing the rows of desks. Robbie watched the two of them advancing sideways towards each other like crabs.

Robbie was inwardly cheering for Chris, who was now taking his side against Dodds. The taunting and threats, the harm he'd caused, the bicycle chain, the rotting squirrel, the wet football and now, more than anything, treating animals so cruelly had Robbie in a rage. He found himself shouting, 'Go for it, Chris!'

The two lads were squaring up to each other, tense, fists ready, chins stuck out.

They were trying to stare each other down. Dodds, not fit but as hefty and thickset as a polar bear. Chris, tall and dark-skinned, wiry and strong, with a laid-back ease about him.

Mr Burton flung the door open and came in to the room. The boys stepped back, still glowering at each other.

'You wait till break! I'll bust your ugly mug,' jeered Dodds out of the side of his mouth.

Chris laughed at him. 'You just try.'

It was hot and thundery by break time. Danger was in the air as boys hurried to the chosen spot, a patch of ground behind the shed next to the playing field. The area they favoured was a neglected corner; nettles, thistles and elderberry bushes were flourishing around the edges of broken tarmac, the scent of the elderflowers hanging in the warm air.

Nothing could be seen from the classrooms or the

staffroom. Feverishly excited, the spectators were shoving each other, pretend kick-boxing and asking the big question. Thunder growled. Robbie felt nervous.

'Hey, Rawdy, who's your man?'

'Chris is my man, that Dodds is a mean one, though.'

'I'm off that Dodds too, but he'll win, you'll see.'

'Sam's betting on Chris.'

'Dodds likes tormenting people.'

'Yeah, but he's funny, I'll go with him.'

Soon there were more than a dozen boys waiting for the stars of the show, Dodds and Chris.

First to arrive was Chris. Robbie tried to catch his eye to show his support. Dodds appeared within seconds, standing at a distance. He had something in his hand. He approached the huddle. There was a gasp as he raised his arm – a bicycle chain.

Now the rules had changed. It would not be a fair fight.

Dodds has got my bicycle chain! He's out to hurt someone. I'm scared Chris'll get hurt, so I've got to help him.

I didn't bring anything with me. I can't go and get anything, there's no time. I'd like to go back to the classroom and get Mr Burton's metal ruler. A hard whack with that would do it. I've got to help Chris somehow. I have to think of something.

The boys were chanting, 'Go, go, go, go!' Glancing round desperately, Robbie's eye fell on Rawdy McCracken who was jumping wildly from one foot to another, waving a can of red lemonade in the air, so wound up he looked ready to send it flying.

Robbie turned quickly back towards the fight. Dodds, his eyes narrowed and glinting with malice, was whirling the chain above his head and advancing on Chris, who was trying to shield his face with his arm. Dodds lashed out. Chris ducked and dodged as well as he could, but the chain caught the side of his shoulder. A groan rose from the boys, followed by a murmur of disapproval. Dodds had drawn the first blood all right. He smiled triumphantly and, with Victor cheering him on, he drew his right arm back to lunge again.

Agile as a monkey, Robbie jumped towards Rawdy, grabbing the can of fizz. Before Rawdy even registered what was happening, Robbie had given the can an extra vigorous shake, pulled the tab and sent a spout of bright red liquid straight into Dodds' face.

There were shouts of laughter, air punches and guffaws.

Dodds, half-blinded, his cheeks dripping with dark pink foam, stumbled and staggered backwards. The bicycle chain fell as he frantically clutched at his streaming eyes. A younger boy darted up, snatched the chain and ran a little way off. Now it would be an even fight.

But it wasn't to be. Dodds caught and jumped on the smaller boy.

This was the signal – with whoops and cries everyone threw themselves into the fray. It was a free-for-all; the bicycle chain passed from hand to hand as Dodds furiously snatched at it, trying to regain control.

Robbie joined in, fighting to stop Dodds getting hold of the bike chain. Lightning flashed and the storm broke in torrents of rain.

When the whistle blew for the end of break, almost every single boy was sopping wet, panting, puce in the face and covered in dirt-encrusted grazes.

When Mr Burton saw the state half his class was in – with ripped clothes, scratches, red swelling eyes and raw knuckles – he went straight to his desk drawer, got out the infamous steel ruler nestled among the empty beer cans and brought it down on the desktop with a crack.

'Who is responsible for this disgrace?' he demanded.

There was complete silence, but the boys were clearly brimming with happiness.

'Speak up! And wipe those silly expressions off your faces,' he roared. 'Or you'll all get a taste of my medicine.'

Robbie thought this was unfair and finally said, 'I suppose it was me, sir. I was trying to get my bicycle chain back.'

Immediately a chorus of voices joined his in support.

'No, sir, it was me!'

'It was me, sir, me!'

CHAPTER 20

To join or not to join?

Robbie was getting his breakfast and had dropped a bowl of cereal on the floor.

'Hey, Robbie, can't you be more careful?' his mum shouted down the stairs.

'Sorry, Mum, but I'll tell you what, not all my friends have to get their own bloody breakfast all the time.'

His mum came down, looking astonished. Robbie didn't move to pick up the pieces. It was the first time he'd questioned the way they lived. And he never ever swore in front of his mum.

'I see,' she said slowly, shaking her head. 'Did you drop it on purpose?'

'Why would I do that?' asked Robbie, meeting her eye.

'Because you're cross with me?' she said.

'Mum, I had a fight at school yesterday, but you never asked me why I had loads of cuts and grazes.'

'What's that you're saying? You had a fight?'

'Yes, there was a fight. The boy who hit me with the football had stolen my bicycle chain and he was using it to fight with.'

'A bicycle chain? And you've been hit with a football?' His mum looked puzzled.

'You didn't know because you weren't there when we went

to the beach. You're never there,' said Robbie. 'It was Dodds, if you want to know, the one who's going to St Mungo's. He's got it in for me, but I'm getting even with him now.' Robbie gave his mum a look that was both fierce and determined and set off for school.

The fight had resulted in one thing – most of the boys now saw Dodds as a dirty fighter. The boys' sense of fairness was strong and with that bicycle chain Dodds had lost the support of the whole class, with the sole exception of Victor. No one joined in now when he goaded the younger boys.

Robbie, on the other hand, had saved the day for Chris, when he could have been badly injured. It was clear he'd gone up in their estimation. When he arrived the next morning one or two said, 'Hey there, maybe see you at break,' or 'All right, Robbie?' or 'Quick-thinking about that lemonade.' At lunch he was invited to share a table with Chris and his friends. They were all still talking about the fight. Robbie was glad to be getting on better with them at last, but he wasn't yet sure he wanted to be one of them. Or was that the only way to survive? He could almost hear his dad's voice.

'Get on with it, Robbie, these will be good friends to have.'

Everyone in our class got detention for fighting. Dodds has been suspended, and he may not come back. Good riddance. I'm safer without Dodds. I used to avoid Chris and his mates too, but they're being nice to me now. It's not the same as being friends, though. Not like the twins and Maddy. They like the same things as me. We get on and they don't make rude jokes all the time. But Chris really helped me with getting Skywalker away. Maybe he could be a good friend.

For the second time Chris invited Robbie to come and sit with him and his mates in the school canteen. By the end of lunch Robbie had heard these boys making jokes about all the teachers, about the food they got at home – who got the most disgusting food, whose older sister had stabbed his little brother in the hand with a fork for taking the last bit of chicken – and about some of the people in their neighbourhoods. Robbie could join in with all of this, although he didn't feel too good saying his mum's food was terrible. Mostly it was fine.

When they started on how they were going to play tricks on some of the younger boys, his heart wasn't in it. But he started to understand something: if you were in a group and the group was doing something, you felt as if you had to join in. He'd been picked on himself and it was awful. He wasn't going to do it to others, just to be included in the group.

But he did join them when they sat down to play cards for money, and he won 50p.

CHAPTER 21

Under the table

Nervous excitement was in the air. The Carrick Hall was stifling, even though the doors had been left wide open. The rows of battered, bright green chairs were filling rapidly. The younger contestants were taking turns to peep round the curtains to see where their parents were sitting. There would be a child finalist and an adult finalist who would compete for the overall title. Jealousy was mounting and costumes were being eyed.

Robbie had refused to wear a pair of blue velvet trousers his aunt had made from the leftover velvet from his mum's dress. He was sitting on a bench at the back of the dressing room wearing what he'd decided was much more appropriate for his performance – a black kilt, a black shirt and a belt with a big silver buckle. He'd eventually persuaded Aunt Mari to make the kilt for him to replace the trousers, after he'd seen Celtic Thunder performing on TV. To complete the outfit he had black knee socks and boots. He'd asked Sandy to accompany him with his guitar.

He'd chosen 'My Love is Like a Red Red Rose' because he loved the melody and it worked well for one person. It suited his voice and he knew people found it beautiful and moving.

The twins were going for a song from *Grease*, and were going to do a bit of dancing to go with it. They were wearing white baseball caps, back to front, sleeveless t-shirts and black jeans. Their sneakers were gleaming white and made their feet look enormous.

It was the young singers first. Robbie saw that Windy Wake had arrived, heightening the air of expectancy in the dressing rooms, which were steeped in a permanent tang of deodorant and hairspray.

Windy retired to a table on the side of the stage, wearing full stage make-up and looking neat in a little black leather jacket with diamante on the collar.

Robbie checked the audience. The hall was packed and noisy. His whole family were there, even Jeff. Sue, the twins' head teacher, looking serene in the front row, was talking to Aunt Mari, who was bending over to hear her in the hubbub. Next to Sue was the mayor, Dev McCleod, and behind them were Maddy's parents and the twins' mum.

One by one the children walked on to the stage to stand in front of the audience and some kind of transformation took place. Overcoming their nerves after one or two bars, they started to belt out their songs and by the end felt exhilarated. Robbie remembered his mum's advice, to sing with real feeling. And with Sandy's tender accompaniment, Robbie could see he'd moved his audience. He and Sandy came down and joined his mum in the audience afterwards. His mum gave him a squeeze. 'Well done, Robbie, well done!'

'I think that went all right,' said Sandy. 'Good news about Skywalker. He's put on a bit of weight and the vet says he's a fine dog. He's young. The police say we can keep him and the Dodds family won't be keeping any pets for a long time.'

They waited impatiently for the next stage of the auditions to start. Robbie glanced up at the judges on the stage. That Rory O'Connor was looking straight at his mum. Robbie found himself taking a strong dislike to him. Something told him this man – so slippery-smooth, so self-important – was bad news.

My mum said she knows that Rory O'Connor from the arts centre. They met because she's working there. Could he be her next boyfriend? I know she'd like one. But I thought it could be Sandy. I much prefer him, he's a great guy. He likes me and he takes care of Skywalker. And he loves singing and dancing, he told me, and so does Mum.

I need to find out more about Rory O'Connor. I'm sure he has secrets. I think he's smarmy and he looks like someone who has something to hide. Maybe I should follow him, see what he's up to.

Maddy sang a song from *My Fair Lady*. Her father put a big armchair on the stage for her, and she wore a big flowery hat with transparent red petals, like a giant poppy. 'All I want is a room somewhere,' she trilled. She did a great cockney accent and she really let go with her voice as she neared the end of the song, belting it out as if she'd been singing for huge audiences all her life.

Windy and SP had each picked their child winners, and they were ready for battle. Once the adult singers had finished, it was time to announce the winners of the two halves of the talent contest. Windy started.

'First the junior contestants. The finalist is—' He stopped and looked about, raising the tension.

'Good luck, Robbie,' whispered Aunt Mari.

'Or rather, I should say the finalists *are* – Maddy *and* Robbie! They're both such fine singers, we couldn't choose between the two of them.'

Thunderous applause broke out across the audience and Robbie could hear cheers and clapping as he tried to take the news in.

'That means you'll have to sing again later, Robbie,' said SP.

'OK,' he said.

He felt so happy that he'd done well, he didn't mind anything.

'Your dad would've been proud of you, Robbie,' said Sandy, who'd just been announced as the finalist from the adult section. Robbie thanked him, but reflected that Sandy hadn't known his dad.

Robbie went to find Maddy. She was jumping with excitement, and the two singers hugged each other joyfully. Over her shoulder, Robbie saw his mum come up on to the stage, smiling up at that Rory O'Connor as if he was her favourite person in the world. And he was smiling back, in a way that made Robbie feel suspicious. It was more of a smirk than a proper smile, he thought, as he saw Rory walk off with his mum.

Wanting to find out more, Robbie decided to take a quick look at the notes O'Connor had been taking. Presumably they were to do with all the different performances. There was a leather-bound notebook and some loose sheets of paper next to the little lamp on the judges' table. He remembered exactly where Rory had been sitting. The other judges were off talking to contestants.

Robbie told Maddy he'd catch up with her soon and went over. But the notes were all written in tiny handwriting and Robbie was highly visible where he was on the stage, so he pretended to knock the notes by mistake. The notebook and papers fell on the floor.

Crouching down as if to pick up the notes, he took shelter under the table, which had a moth-eaten red woollen cloth over the front so no one could see him there. He started to read the notes. They weren't interesting, just about the singers and performers. He saw that Rory didn't like the timbre of Maddy's voice. I wonder what it's got to do with timber? he thought.

There was movement, and Robbie saw legs and shoes right in front of his face as the judges all came back and sat down. He admired SP's studded cowboy boots. But how to get out from underneath the table? There was nothing for it, he'd just have to climb out. He stuck the notebook inside his shirt, picked up the notes and emerged from under the cloth. The audience all laughed. Rory O'Connor looked rather annoyed. Robbie said, as convincingly as he could, 'I was just picking up some bits of paper that got dropped.' He placed them on the table and ran off the stage, the notebook still nestling against his skin.

He'd hardly had time to get off the stage when the judges called him back. 'You'll be on in ten minutes, Robbie,' said SP, showing him the smile that had melted hundreds of hearts harder than Robbie's.

'This is your big moment, hon, show us what you can do.'

They'd rather sprung that on him. The notebook would have to wait. He found a quiet spot in the boys' dressing room where he could concentrate on the singing.

He had a couple of songs he liked. He decided on 'Over the Rainbow', something he used to sing with his mum. Judy Garland was supposed to be a very young girl when she sang it so it worked for a young voice. His mum had sung it at the very first auditions. They both knew it well.

He was ready when the judges summoned him. The three of them sat on the dark stage, surrounded by shadows, with a small table lamp in front of them. A spotlight shone on Robbie, who stood alone. Maddy and Sandy had already performed their second songs. The microphone buzzed. The audience shuffled.

He could just make out Rory searching underneath his heap of notes and then bending to look under the table. Now he was looking at Robbie. Would he guess about the missing notebook?

Robbie tried to concentrate and opened his mouth to sing. He faltered. The leather diary was warm and stuck to the skin of his stomach. He felt hot and ill.

'Take your time,' cooed SP soothingly. 'Start again when you're ready.'

Rory was staring right at him with undisguised hostility. Robbie stood hypnotised by that deeply unfriendly gaze. He could barely remember what he was supposed to be doing. With a huge effort, he dragged his eyes away, straightened his back and started his song. It was hard, but the words came flowing back to him and he sang out. The audience were ecstatic.

The judges put their heads together. Robbie could just make out what they were saying and wondered whether he was still meant to be standing there. But they hadn't told him to go, so he listened. With what sounded to Robbie like artificial enthusiasm, Rory said, 'That Maddy! What a voice, what a talent, *and* she has the confidence to carry it off.'

'And the same applies to Robbie,' said Windy Wake. 'But those two kids have plenty of time in front of them. Sandy's got a stunning voice, and he needs to start taking himself seriously now, or it may be too late for him.'

'On the nail, man, sure thing, that voice of his is like warm peanut butter,' said SP. 'Let's give the man a boost now and maybe he can do something with it. I'm voting for him.'

When the judges made their announcement, the audience, all dressed up for the dance afterwards, cheered and called out for Sandy – he was a very popular man. So Sandy was the winner and was asked to sing again.

Poor Maddy burst into tears and then, with a clear struggle, she managed to act as if she was pleased for Sandy. It was a blow, too, for Robbie the singer. He could see that his family were deflated and he'd especially wanted to win for his dad. But Robbie the detective, who'd been trying to think of a way to find out more about Rory, had other things to take his mind off the disappointment. There was, for instance, the notebook.

Robbie was sitting at the back of the hall at a table with Fay and the twins. He was holding the notebook. It was black leather and had a small gold snake stamped on the front.

'What's that you've got there?' said Harry.

'It's that Rory O'Connor's notebook,' whispered Robbie. 'I want to find out about him, because I think he may be dodgy, and he's got his eye on my mum.'

'Your mum's lucky,' said Fay. 'He seems like a very clever, interesting man. He's the one making something out of the arts centre. This evening was all his idea.'

'Well, I don't like him.'

'But Robbie,' said Fay, 'your mum might like him. Don't you think it's up to her who she likes?'

Robbie looked down at the little leather notebook. He decided to keep his view on preferring Sandy secret. She'd only go and say that it wasn't up to him.

'What's in the notebook, Robbie?' said Harry, when they'd stepped on to the floor and were out of earshot.

'I'll tell you later when I've looked,' said Robbie. 'Let's find someone to dance with.'

'I'll dance with Harry,' said Charlie, laughing.

'So will I!' said Robbie. And the three of them were soon dancing together with Maddy and her friend Flora. The hall was packed and the dance was a great success.

I'm in bed and I'm looking at this notebook. It's some kind of diary, I think, but it's not interesting. It just says 'lunch Roger M' and 'coffee Rose L'. Hey! That's Mum. That was last week. And here it says 'dinner Rose' and a name that sounds like a restaurant. It's in a couple of days. I might ask Aunt Mari what she thinks of the restaurant he's taking her to.

I wish I'd won the talent contest for Mum, and for Dad as well, but I was glad Sandy got it. I got into the finals but I was put off by the way that O'Connor man looked at me. I could see his face all in shadows from the lamp; he looked sinister.

There's nothing much in this diary. I think I'll give it back to him. In the front it's got his address. I could go there and see where he lives. But maybe I'd better not. Mum wouldn't like me spying on her new 'friend'.

I talked to Sandy at the hall and he told me Sky is getting better and it's a cert he'll be a champion.

I keep on remembering how sad the animals were in Dodds' yard. I hope Mrs Dodds doesn't come after Skywalker.

Back at school Robbie was looking forward to lunch for once. He wanted to catch up with Chris. Dodds hadn't been in class and he wondered what had happened. Chris had saved him a place and was brimming with awesome news. After the bicycle chain episode, Mr Burton had made it his business to look in everyone's locker, not realising that Robbie had his chain back. He was determined to find the culprits.

When he came to Dodds' locker he'd found not only traces of grease from the chain but heaps of things he'd stolen. There were watches, a glossy book on reptiles, a cool pair of brand-new trainers, the school dartboard which had gone missing earlier that term and a teapot from the canteen. The police had been called and because there'd been a lot of other problems – at home, at school and with the police – he'd been placed in a special boarding school for troubled teenagers.

He was not coming back.

Victor, sitting alone, was a pitiful sight. His hero and protector had been toppled, the reign of terror over. He'd have to look for new allies. So far there were no offers.

Watching from Chris's table, Robbie felt almost sorry for Victor, but he wanted to hear more about the Dodds family, so he stayed put.

Chris's mother had heard from her friend Mrs Gunawardener that Mrs Dodds, who they all reckoned was the neighbour from hell, had received a fine and community service and was now home. She had triumphantly returned and she had somehow, unbelievably, got hold of a tiger cub and was making money from people having their photographs taken with it.

She kept it in the old privy in her yard.

'What do you say, Robbie, shall we let it free?' said Chris.

'What would happen to it if we did?' said Robbie.

'It would roam the streets and climb the lamp posts to look at the moon,' said one of Chris's friends.

'It would go round biting people's throats out,' said another.

'It would become a bus driver and everyone would wonder why the passengers kept on disappearing,' said Robbie.

They decided to keep an eye on the situation.

Robbie had been on his bike to see Aunt Mari.

She'd welcomed him in and he found Aunt Lizzie sitting at the kitchen table with a mug of coffee. She was telling Aunt Mari about Jeff, who was at home on leave until next week. Robbie saw an opportunity.

'Could Jeff come over and look after me when Mum goes out for the evening next Wednesday?' he said, guilelessly. 'She's going to a place called the Post House. It's in River Street.'

'Really?' said Aunt Mari. 'That's a very posh place, who's she going with?'

'Oh, some man, I think,' said Robbie vaguely. 'She didn't say. Not Sandy, anyway.'

'I'm sure Jeff can come over,' said Aunt Lizzie. 'He'd love to, he's very fond of you, Robbie.'

'Oh good, that's great. Aunt Mari?' he said, changing tack.

'Yes, Robbie?'

'Do you know Sue, the head teacher of St Mungo's, where I'm going next term?'

'Yes, I do, she's a fine teacher. You're so lucky to be going there, you did so well.'

'Well, I was wondering if she knows that the other person who was coming from my school, Dodds, won't be able to come now,' he said.

'Oh, why's that?' said Aunt Mari.

'He's been sent to a school where he'll get special teaching because of all the trouble he's been in.'

'Oh, Lord,' she said, frowning. 'What a disaster! Honest to God, that school of yours – it's not much of a start in life for any child.' She went over to the sink, and stood looking out of the window. When she turned she had tears in her eyes. 'Sorry, Robbie, I haven't given you anything to drink. Are you thirsty? A cup of tea?'

'No, thank you. I was just thinking...'

'Oh, yes, what were you thinking?' she asked suspiciously. 'You sound like you have a plan.'

He had. He thought that his dad had wanted him to make friends at his school. He'd always told Robbie they were good friends to have. Well, he'd finally found someone he liked there, but now he was going to leave and go to St Mungo's. Robbie had worked out that he had two choices: stay at his old school or take the friend with him.

'There's a boy in my class who is very, very clever, but his mum doesn't have anyone or any money and she has a baby. He helps her look after the baby,' said Robbie.

'Oh, that's hard on him,' said Aunt Mari.

'Yes, but he would be a good person to go to St Mungo's,' said Robbie. 'He's called Chris O'Dowd.'

It was late. Jeff and Robbie were playing cards. Jeff was great at keeping Robbie amused but not good at getting him off to bed. His mother came in with Aunt Mari and Brendan Bentham and sat down with them in the kitchen.

Robbie saw his mother throwing one of her high heels across the room and then the other, and he went and stood near her. She gave him a hug. He thought the date must have gone badly wrong, which was what he wanted, but he felt sorry for his mum and hugged her back. She gave him a squeeze.

'Time for bed, Robbie,' she said.

'OK,' said Robbie. 'Goodnight, everyone. Bye, Jeff. Don't forget we're going to look at that boat tomorrow.'

Jeff let himself out and Robbie disappeared up the stairs, but paused halfway up to listen.

He heard his mum saying, 'I'm massively glad you turned up, Mari, but what a thing, us both going to the same restaurant.'

'Yes, wasn't it?' said Aunt Mari. 'A bit of a surprise to see you with Rory O'Connor, though.'

'What a mistake.' He heard his mum let out a deep sigh. 'Total control freak. First of all he told me what to eat, and he ordered artichokes and then octopus, two things I've never eaten – a sort of test, I suppose. Then he started telling me how to eat the artichoke! He said, "You're making a terrible job of that, this is how I do it." He insisted that pearl earrings would look better than my gold hoops and that he would buy me some, and then he wasn't sure he liked me in blue; black would be more sophisticated. After that he drank a lot of wine and talked non-stop about what a big shot he is. You wouldn't believe how conceited the man is.'

'What kind of conceited?' asked Brendan.

'Well, he kept saying things like, "I'm the kind of man who knows how to make things happen," and, "I've got great schemes afoot." He actually said, "Watch this space, I'll soon be the wealthiest man in Ulster." It was hard to keep a straight face. Then he capped it all by saying, "You just wait until my ship comes in." Luckily you two came along and sat down with us at that point. Did you see? He was furious!'

Robbie heard Brendan's voice.

'Well, when I saw you there with him I wasn't happy. I don't know him well but I *can* tell you that he went out with a colleague of mine and she said he was a nasty bit of work – no way you could know that, Rose, so don't blame yourself.'

Robbie heard Aunt Mari saying, 'I'll go and check on Robbie, shall I?'

He hurried up to his room and jumped into bed.

Just in time. Aunt Mari appeared in the doorway.

'I keep asking myself something,' she said. 'How the heck did you know the name and address of that restaurant, Robbie?'

'Not sure,' he said as casually as he could. 'Must have read about it somewhere.'

'But how did you know your mum was going there tonight?'

'I saw it written down somewhere, I think,' he said.

'Well, it was bang on, I'm glad you told me. It was a lovely restaurant and we all had a good time.' Robbie raised an eyebrow at her lies, but she didn't seem to notice. 'I just wondered whatever made you come and tell me about it?'

'Oh... You know...' Robbie started to yawn, and pretended to be drifting off to sleep.

CHAPTER 22

Tiger, tiger

Robbie was guiding Aunt Mari as she drove down some unfamiliar streets. There they were, the boarded-up shops and the cars with no tyres.

Robbie was taking Aunt Mari to see the O'Dowd family. They reached the corner of the street where Billy Dodds' house faced Chris's, the two lines of terraced houses looking at each other. They parked the car and knocked on the door. The door was opened by a thin, young black woman with a ponytail. Over her shoulder was a towel, and she held a small baby in one arm and in the other hand a bottle of milk.

'Have you come about the Dodds family?' she said, excitedly. 'The racket that comes from over there these days, you wouldn't believe! It's got much worse. The yapping, howling, screeching – what with my baby and their animals, I get no sleep. Sounds as if she's got more critters than ever. People have been asking me all sorts of questions about them.'

She gestured to them to come in. 'Mina Gunawardener thinks they've got all their animals back! But I think she's just gone out and got new ones, and started again. Can you credit it?'

'Well, that *is* strange,' said Aunt Mari as Robbie followed her in to the house. 'My nephew, Robbie here, tells me he's a friend of your son. I actually came to talk about Chris.'

'Oh, yes?' said Chris's mother. Robbie thought she looked less friendly. There was a wary look on her face. 'What's this, then, has he been bunking off?'

'I'm not from the school, but it is *about* school. Can we sit down?'

'Sure you can. This is Bunny, she's three months old. Doing well, thank God. Well, that Dodds boy, at least he's gone. He and my Chris never really got on. My name's Jacky, by the way.'

'I'm Mari. I haven't met Chris yet.'

'Oh, he's still kipping. He helped me out, gave the baby her bottle at five this morning. I was banjaxed. He's a good son. I was young when I had him, he's almost like a little brother to me.'

Aunt Mari smiled and gave the baby a finger to hold on to.

'I wanted to ask you,' she said, 'whether you're happy with Chris's school? Is he happy there?'

'Will I get you a cup of tea?' said Jacky, narrowing her eyes. 'Now, why is it you're here exactly?'

Aunt Mari, perched on a precariously wobbly chair, was trying her best to explain about the possibility of an assisted place at St Mungo's coming up, when they heard a deep growling noise. Screams split the air.

They went to the window but could see nothing, yet the noise had come from just across the road. Robbie could see that the yard of the Dodds' house was fenced and there was now barbed wire along the top.

Footsteps thumped overhead and Chris, in a t-shirt and underpants, came crashing down the stairs.

'There's animals fighting over there or something,' he said. 'But I can't really see what's going on. Sounds like they're tearing each other to pieces.'

Aunt Mari took Robbie and hurried across the road. Chris grabbed some trousers and ran to the gate of the yard. He gave Robbie a leg up again. He could just see over the top.

Thrashing around in the dirt and trodden cabbage leaves was Mrs Dodds! A young tiger was on top of her, pinning her down, threatening sounds coming from deep in its throat. Teeth bared, it was lashing at her arm with its claws in a frenzy.

Mrs Dodds was trying to get up, but the young tiger had badly torn her arms and mauled her hands as she held them up to protect her face.

'Help!' she cried. 'Help me!'

But the gate was now padlocked with a brand-new, massive motorbike chain and there was no way to get in.

Across the street, Robbie could hear Chris's mum calling to Chris to take care. Robbie tried to describe to Aunt Mari what he'd seen and she got out her phone to telephone the police and ambulance, while Chris ran back to his house and grabbed a chair.

Robbie and Chris managed to climb and push and pull each other up to the top of the gate and get into the yard.

Things weren't looking good for Mrs Dodds, but Chris found an old wooden broom and grabbed it.

'Do you reckon she's worth it?' he muttered to Robbie,

before he jumped at the growling tiger with the broomstick, jabbing at it, while Robbie picked up an enamel bowl of mucky water and threw it over the animal and Mrs Dodds. To their surprise, it let go and retreated, still snarling. It slunk to the old privy where it shook itself, dirty water flying everywhere. They slammed the door and bolted it.

By now the commotion had drawn a good crowd of passers-by and neighbours who were talking excitedly in the street outside. Two or three local children, seeing some fun, started to throw sticks, stones, tin cans, anything they could pick up, over the fence.

Robbie watched as they rained down on the great Mrs Marvella herself, flat on her back in the dirt, bleeding and soaking wet.

Robbie and Chris tried to get the woman back on her feet. But now the attack was over, she was wheezing badly and seemed unwilling to get up, even with the boys' help. Robbie thought they should wait for the ambulance.

Two frightened little faces, peeping out of the back door of the Dodds' house, caught his eye.

Aunt Mari had managed to stop the kids throwing missiles and she was trying to find someone with a bolt cutter so they could get inside the yard. She shouted to Robbie to ask what was happening.

'We're fine, but Mrs Dodds is still on the ground. We can't get her up.'

'The ambulance will be here soon,' called Aunt Mari.

Robbie went to ask one of the little girls at the back door

to look after her mum and then followed Chris through the house to open the front door, ready for the paramedics. The onlookers came crowding round, shoving their way forwards, desperate to come inside and see for themselves what was going on.

'No, please don't go in,' said Robbie, trying to push them away. A police siren sounded, coming fast towards them. The crowd stepped back.

The police edged heavily through the dark, narrow corridor of the house to the yard. Robbie could see a large cage through the open back doors of their truck. He followed them through to the backyard where Mrs Dodds was still lying on the ground. Nearby, Robbie could see her two little girls sobbing.

Robbie thought the officers – armed with tranquilliser guns and long poles with wire nooses – looked like alien storm troopers with their black, padded clothing and their heads encased in cage-like masks. The snarling tiger was captured and tranquillised. Once it was still, they took it off, leaving the remaining officers to deal with Mrs Dodds.

When she saw them she groaned, 'For mercy's sake, give me a cup of tea, I'm dying here, I'm torn to pieces, bleeding to death, can't you see? Get on with it, won't you?'

'You just lie there, Mrs Dodds, and keep calm,' said the police officer.

The paramedics arrived and kneeled down in the muck of the yard, making soothing conversation to calm the wounded woman as they took her blood pressure and pulse. That done, she suddenly raised her head and lumbered to her feet, soaked in dirty water and covered in mire, and started shouting at them. Robbie was shocked at her sudden recovery.

'You get out of here at once, do you hear me? The lot of you, what're you doing here on my property? This is private, have you got a warrant? Course you bloody don't, so leave now.'

A police officer came over.

'You've got a record, Mrs Dodds, and a dangerous animal just attacked you, so don't make more trouble for yourself. Let them take you to hospital and sort out your arm.'

She looked at her arm, gashed and bloody.

'I'm going indoors,' she said, 'you can all bugger off.'

One of the paramedics said, 'Please, Mrs Dobbs, listen—'

'Don't call me that! Where's yer respect?' she shouted. 'It's *Dodds*, and I'm not bloody going anywhere.'

'Listen to me. There's the possibility of blood poisoning or tetanus. You must come with us – is there someone, a neighbour, who can look after your little girls?'

The danger was over. The excitement was over. The young tiger, tranquillised and caged, had been removed to a happier home at a nearby zoo. Mrs Dodds, untranquillised, uncaged and still raging, had also been removed. Which of them had been more hostile and uncooperative it would be hard to say, thought Robbie. He and Aunt Mari and the two little Dodds children were sitting in Jacky's kitchen. Chris was making tea.

'Thanks for letting us bring the girls over,' said Aunt Mari.

'Sure, the poor little scraps. Haven't they only just got

over the last time they saw the police in their yard,' said Jacky. 'They need a break, they're having it rough.'

That tiger was close; I could see it had golden eyes. I suspect it wanted to kill someone if it could. Probably Mrs Dodds, for preference. Lucky Chris was there and we managed to get it off her or it might have been curtains for the great Mrs Marvella. I'm glad the police took all her animals away for rehoming.

I can see Chris has to do a lot for his mum at the moment. He's looking out for her. She doesn't have anyone else.

I'm not the only one. It's not just me. No one round here has a dad. No one has a perfect life. Or a perfect mum. I wouldn't want Mrs Dodds for a mum. Poor Dodds, I almost feel sorry for him. I thought everyone else had the sort of family that I'd like to have. But it isn't like that. Some of them have a worse time.

I feel so bad about losing my dad. Mum says he cared about me, that's why he was hard on me and tried to put the fear of God into me. I loved my dad, but when he was angry with me I usually tried to stay out of his way by disappearing to my secret place in the woods.

I've tried to fight the tears, but I can't. I can't get my dad back and see him again.

But we were all right, weren't we, Dad?

CHAPTER 23

Silent stalkers

On the first day of the autumn term, the two boys met up with their bikes at Arlen ferry port. They wore their comfortable old grey school uniforms. They were cycling companionably, side by side, along the overgrown country lane that meandered towards St Mungo's, when a string of cars drove up behind and pushed irritably past them. They moved over, brushing the grasses as they wobbled towards the ditch. Robbie suddenly began to get a prickle in his skin; it felt a bit like danger. His mouth felt dry and he almost turned round, but Chris was riding on, confident and cheerful.

He calmed down as they approached the school. After all, he did have a couple of friends there. That should make it easier.

They pedalled up the drive. Two more cars swished by, pulling up with a scrunch of gravel in front of the big country house that was home to the school. Chris approached a boy scrambling out of one of the cars.

'Is there a bike shed?' he said.

'Over there.' The boy pointed. 'In front of those stables.'

'Come on, Toby,' called an impatient voice from inside the car. 'Get on with it, in you go. No time for chatting.'

Toby shrugged apologetically and trotted into the school. The car drove off with a lurch, almost making Chris tip over.

'Cool yer jets!' he shouted in disgust after the departing car.

They parked their bikes in a deserted stable yard, and then took a deep breath. Leaving the sunlight behind, they stepped into the dark hall of the school, dwarfed by the lofty space.

Buoyed up by each other's company, they followed the last stragglers into the unfamiliar assembly room. Hundreds of eyes turned towards them, as the two boys, the only ones wearing school uniform, hovered.

There were no empty chairs to be seen and Robbie was beginning to feel awkward when he saw a hand wave to them. It was Maddy!

'Robbie, come over here,' she said, and they found themselves sitting with Maddy, her friend Flora, and several other girls who studied them slyly out of the corners of their eyes. Chris, in his shabby grey suit and tie, his hair in cornrows, sat there looking around, checking out, Robbie suspected, these new schoolmates smiling at him shyly.

The hall was hushed and waiting. At the front sat the teachers – there was Sue, relaxed and smiling, flanked by a bald Indian man who Robbie recognised as Surid, the school bursar. They'd been introduced when he'd visited school with his mum. And here, Robbie noticed, sitting expectantly in their seats, were children of all races. At his last school, Chris had been the only boy of colour. He had quite sensibly taken up boxing.

Some of the girls already knew Robbie. Maddy's friend Flora had been at the talent contest in the Carrick Hall when Robbie and Maddy had shared the second prize. Maddy told Robbie that the girls saw him as a bit of a star. Things were starting well. Sue, the head teacher, was welcoming everyone back and introducing the newcomers. She finished by saying that there would be a Christmas show of some sort, and she'd let them know what had been chosen by the end of the week.

As the welcome ended, a neat boy of about Robbie's age, wearing jeans and a clean, brushed-cotton plaid shirt, came up to show them to their new classroom.

They followed him along the length of a short corridor smelling of coffee and lined with bright papier mâché masks.

The last room was theirs; the boy, who seemed quite friendly, introduced himself as Flipper. He admitted he was really called Rupert, but had disowned the name. He waved and walked away. They could hear his retreating footsteps on the wooden floor of the corridor as they stood in the doorway, looking in at their new classmates with sinking hearts.

It's all so different, but I'm glad I got away from the old school, and from that bully Dodds who hated me. I'm so pleased that Aunt Mari managed to arrange for Chris to take his school place and come to St Mungo's with me instead.

I'll wait until break time and then I'll go and look for the twins. Chris and me have been put in a different class to them for some subjects. We both passed the exam to be here, so we can't be far behind. But there are a few subjects where we need to catch up. Anyway, I know about different things to them. I know about real things. Like how to use binoculars. How to mend a bike, and put up a tent. I can help Sandy with his boat. I know the Bible – practically all of it. And I know how to be a detective; I'm good at hiding and I can track people and follow them without them knowing. And I have my singing.

And Chris, he knows everything about looking after people and how to feed a baby and change it. And he's a great boxer, he really knows how to fight. He's taller than anyone else in the class.

I'm dying to meet the music teacher. I can't wait to learn the keyboard and Chris wants to learn guitar, so we can do our own music, like Robbie Williams. We can start our own group.

Sandy thinks it's a good idea. He says life without music would be like a pub with no beer.

Robbie sat at his desk in the new classroom and watched his classmates chatting amiably. The teacher came in, smiling. She actually seemed as if she was glad to see them all. Farewell, Mr Burton, unwashed, wrecked and ready to lash out at the first person who caught his attention.

Miss Bryony was a tall Australian lady with thick, bunchy blonde hair, chopped off under the ears, and an open, freckled face. Their first class was natural history and environment.

She handed out notebooks and books of animal drawings.

Asking them to find the right page, she started to talk.

'Do you all know what a reptile is? Snakes are reptiles and so are crocs. We have a lot of crocs in Australia. We have salties, who live in seawater, and freshies, who live in freshwater dams, creeks and lagoons.' She held up a picture of a croc's open jaws. 'See those little dark spots on her head? They're sensors. When she's underwater she can detect the ripple from a drop of water running off an animal's muzzle, the dip of an oar or a splashing swimmer – she senses them from far off.'

Robbie was transfixed. This was interesting. And she was telling it like a story.

'Our Mrs Croc's a silent stalker, she moves stealthily, then ... smack!' She clapped her hands together. Robbie almost jumped. Miss Bryony smiled fiercely.

'That wily old croc rears right up out of the water, one whole ton of sheer muscle, and grabs her dinner, shaking, biting and crushing it, and dragging it under the water to drown.'

There were some cries of 'No!' but Miss Bryony said, 'Sorry, kids, that's the way nature works. Mrs Croc's not cruel, she's only doing what crocs naturally do.'

'Snakes are stealthy too,' she continued, 'another silent stalker, and they can do cunning things to attract their prey.' She showed them another picture. 'Some of them eat birds; Slippery Sid here entices them out of the sky by wiggling the tip of his tail to look like a juicy worm.'

Robbie put his hand up and Miss Bryony smiled at him and nodded.

'Can they kill a person, the snakes?' he asked.

'They can. They're a big menace in Africa, and in Brazil they have pit vipers called lanceheads. They're one of the most dangerous snakes in the world. 'There's a deserted island off the Brazilian coast called Snake Island. All the people left because there's just thousands of these vipers. The lighthouse keeper and his whole family, the last people left on the island, were killed by a swarm of them as they tried to board a boat to get away. Legend says they were introduced to the island to protect buried treasure. There's a rumour that smugglers still risk their lives to capture them. They're protected, worth a shedload of money. The venom is used to make medicine.'

'Do *all* snakes have venom – the ones that are meant to have it, I mean?' asked Robbie.

'No,' said Miss Bryony. 'Occasionally a venomous snake doesn't have the venom it's meant to. But I wouldn't want to take the risk! Would you?'

Good-humoured laughter filled the room. Robbie enjoyed the nature class immensely and when asked to write what he'd heard, he wrote enthusiastically, and finished with 'Only a desperado would approach Snake Island, but woe to him if he lands his boat there. The snakes will always win.' He felt quite pleased and decided he wasn't going to make a fuss about changing to a higher form just yet – he liked Miss Bryony a lot.

At the end of the morning he took Chris with him to find the twins. They followed the smell of roast chicken, wafting temptingly through the corridors. The twins were already sitting in the dining room, surrounded by other children. They waved at Robbie.

'We kept you a place,' called Charlie.

But they'd saved only one place, and Robbie wanted to find somewhere he could sit with Chris.

They chose, again, to sit with Maddy and her friends. The girls were pleased to make room for them.

Chris queued up with the girls. He stared hungrily at the lunch counter, anxious there'd be nothing left when he got there. But the two dinner ladies had a bottomless pot that could never run out. As fast as they were emptied, more tin dishes loaded with chicken and roast potatoes came out of the kitchen.

When his turn came, Chris piled his plate with chicken, spuds and peas. As they sat down he looked at Robbie and gave him a thumbs up. The girls watched fascinated as he emptied his plate and went back for more. Flora whispered, 'That was crazy. It looks as if he's never eaten a proper meal before.' Robbie knew she wasn't far off the truth.

Maddy was talking about the acting classes she'd taken in the holidays. All the girls were encouraging her to tell them more, and she, like Miss Bryony, was a good storyteller and had no inhibitions – she was more than ready to talk about herself and the glamour of the drama school, with its real stage and red velvet curtains.

This was a new world for the two boys, whose school experience so far had been raw boy culture, based as it was on little more than harsh, rule-bound discipline. Now they were taking in the new, friendly regime in great gulps. But Robbie wasn't yet sure what to expect, or how to behave in this unknown terrain. Like the wild creature stepping close to the billabong for a drink, he was watchful for any lurking threat.

Robbie got home full of his day and his mum enjoyed the stories. He went to bed feeling his first day hadn't been too bad. But as dusk fell, the weather turned muggy and a thunderstorm rolled and rumbled over the town and finally exploded over their house like bombs going off. Robbie, trying to sleep, tossed and turned in the dark. The flickering lightning got on his nerves and midge bites on his legs were driving him mad. He tried singing 'Amazing Grace' to himself and, before long, he was floating under the moon on a darkened sea, which rippled around him as if inky wavelets gently patted the boat to move it forwards in the still night air. An island lay before him. A black tangle of trees reared up as the ghostly boat approached. There lay a moonlit beach. He could smell something rotten in the air. It reminded him of the dead squirrel in his locker. His skin prickled. As he watched, the sky lightened to a pale primrose colour and flocks of bright blue birds started to fly over.

He was tempted to land but the putrid atmosphere told him there was danger afoot and he stayed on board. Some of the birds were landing in the trees, and seconds later he heard terrible cries of pain from the undergrowth.

The birds fell quiet and he saw, from the edge of the jungle, a mass of writhing shapes. Swarms of snakes, pale gold in colour, were slithering towards him. They were barely visible on the pale yellow sand. He tried to push the boat away from the beach but it was stuck.

He saw Sandy rowing in a small boat. As he came nearer he shouted a warning to Robbie.

'This is Snake Island, beware!'

A clap of thunder, followed by torrential rain, brought Robbie back to reality and he woke drenched in the sweat of fear.

CHAPTER 24

In the cellar

Robbie asked if he could have keyboard lessons. The school's answer was no – they'd tried them once but preferred to teach on the piano. Lots of musicians had started that way, so Robbie didn't complain. But his first piano lesson was not a success.

Miss La Violetta sat next to him as he perched on the slippery leatherette piano stool in the school's music rooms. He ran his fingers up and down the keys in a trance. This was his dream. For a moment he felt like a rock star. To use sounds and tones and rhythms and patterns of notes to make a song – what a good feeling that would be.

Slowly, he became aware that the billowy woman sitting beside him, smelling powerfully of Bounty bars, was speaking to him. In a gentle voice, which nevertheless conveyed that there was to be no argument, she insisted that he had to learn scales and how to read music.

That evening he made a toasted sandwich and went to sit at the kitchen table, just as Sandy arrived with the dog, who was now glossily well and fit. Skywalker needed a lot of walking so Sandy often walked over in the early evenings.

'How's St Blingo's today?' he asked Robbie, yawning, tired from his day on the boat.

Robbie sighed. 'It's OK, but they haven't got a keyboard I

can use, they've got a piano. And I have to learn how to read notes. It's like having to learn to read again. It's not as much fun as I thought.'

Sandy looked deep in thought for a moment, and then said, 'Say nothing, but if you can surprise your mum by learning to read music, I'll get you your own keyboard. Then you can do all your own stuff as well. It won't do you any harm and it could come in dead useful. I often wish I could read music. I've been getting gigs with other musicians since that talent contest, see, but I can't read a note and that's not good enough.'

Robbie's grandfather had been a singer and a genius fiddle player, playing in all the local bars, and it seemed the gene had passed on to Robbie. With Sandy's encouragement, he soon picked up how to make a tune, and the slow progress with reading music was balanced by the ease with which he held a tune once he'd heard it.

During break times he and Chris went exploring and discovered, behind a large heavy door in a damp back corridor, worn stone steps down to the old cellars under the school.

Where once it had all been a bustle, Robbie and Chris found dark, neglected old kitchens and pantries, some with big fireplaces whose chimneys were still black with soot. This was where all the cooking had been done and where the numerous domestics, cooks, parlour maids and bootboys had once lived out their lives. St Mungo's had been the family home of the head teacher's grandmother.

'This is cool,' said Robbie. 'Whole families could live down here.'

Cobwebby windows, high up in the walls, let in a dim, soft light, half obscured by fluffy stems of rosebay willowherb growing outside at ground level. The pervasive weed pressed, rotting, against the window panes, adding to the feel of decay. There were numerous shadowy wine cellars, musty and humid, and a vast, stone-flagged larder or perhaps a dairy, with black slate shelves.

Robbie surveyed crowds of unwashed paintbrushes in sticky tins and jars, and several paint-splashed chests of drawers filled with tattered old sketchbooks, paints and charcoal. This must have been an art studio at one time. His eyes lit on something in the corner. What was an ironing board doing down there? He took a closer look. It wasn't an ironing board at all. Under a filthy plastic cover was an electronic keyboard, plugs dangling.

'Hey, Chris! Have a look at this, this must be the one they threw out. I wonder if it still works?'

'Only one way to find out,' said Chris, plugging it into a dubious-looking wall socket. Coloured lights lit up on the control panel. After fiddling with the switches and plugging in the microphone, Robbie started picking out a tune.

That autumn term the school cellars were busy again, adopted as a refuge by Robbie and his friends. They discovered an old electric pottery kiln and the twins brought in sausages to cook in it, instead of the pots it was meant for. They found a table and some old folding chairs and made themselves comfortable in their own way. Robbie frequently tried out his music on the keyboard and Chris kept his guitar down there, hidden behind some easels, and every day he was getting closer to a sound he liked.

One lunch break, Robbie and Chris sneaked down with the twins. The kiln was heating up nicely and, as well as small sausages, Fay had provided a sliced white loaf, the kind that never goes stale. They were busy getting ready to make toast and fry the bangers. Robbie saw Chris start and glance up at the window. There was a slight noise of crunching gravel, high up outside. Following Chris's gaze, Robbie strained to see. Was it a head he could see through those weeds? Yes. A pair of eyes was watching them.

'Did you see? At the window?' Chris said, pointing at the shadowy window. But by that time, the figure had ducked away and was gone.

It was a cool September evening. The sun was low and around it the little clouds bloomed a gorgeous, silky red. Robbie and Chris were riding side by side on their bikes.

'I miss my mates,' said Chris. 'I'm meeting them at the chippie. Wanna come?'

'Sure,' said Robbie. 'I'll just tell my mum. She'll be fine, I'll do the homework tomorrow.'

A dizzying smell of greasy frying fat hit Robbie from two streets away. The chippie, painted a glowing lime green inside, was neon-lit, steamy and packed with bodies.

Bathed in the green glare stood red Formica tables, on which packets of fish and chips were unfurled for the boys to add salt and vinegar, ketchup and brown sauce. Here, Chris and the other boys met together regularly, shared chips, had a chat and then headed off home with the family dinner congealing in its oily, crackling paper under their jackets. It was the first time Robbie had joined them.

'Hey, Chris, you posh wee git,' said his friend, Rawdy. 'How's St Blingo's?'

Robbie had always thought it was just Sandy who called it that.

The chat today was all about Dodds, the tormentor. It was now common knowledge that the strict school Billy Dodds had been sent to was Coolin House, where he'd joined his older brother. Chris's friends, tough, cheerful and stolid, relished sharing the details of Dodds' downfall with Robbie.

'He got what he asked for, end of story,' said Chris, his mouth full of chips. His friends agreed. Robbie looked away, confused. Dodds had made his life a misery, but to be sent away from your school and friends... That was hard.

CHAPTER 25

The blue guitar

I'm getting on all right at school. It's not boring because
they have all sorts of things for us to do, which they call
'outdoor work', so we're outside a lot, which I like. I helped
to mend an old tractor and get the engine going again,
which was great.

Now we're constructing a carnival animal out of willow
wands and paper. Me and the twins are building a gigantic
white ant which is taller than we are. We can pick it up and
get underneath to carry it. Other boys and girls are working
on different insects. There'll be a procession of them – beetles
and dragonflies and other things. I'll have a torch to light up
my ant from inside. Once we had to stay late for a poetry
walk, which happened after it got dark. That was fun. But
most days we go on a bike ride after school.

Me and Chris are the only ones who come to school
on bikes. Everyone else comes to school by car and their
parents pick them up afterwards. But we go off on our
own. I'll be going home with Chris today. I'm going to
watch the house across the road from him, where Billy
Dodds lived. His mum is cruel. She never looks after her
animals or feeds them properly. Now she's banned from
keeping them and the police are supposed to have their

eye on her. But she still keeps getting more. I heard it's peacocks this time.

Robbie was at Chris's house. It was hot and windy. From the bedroom window, Robbie scanned the house across the road. He'd brought his binoculars and he could see dust devils rising in the air and whirling round the yard. There were no creatures to be seen. Detectives aren't supposed to give up. Chris wandered off but Robbie waited. After a while, out of the house came a boy of about sixteen, with a narrow face, pinched and sallow. He went towards the old privy.

He was hauling something heavy behind him. A holdall?

'Chris, Chris, come here, who's that? In the yard?'

Chris looked over Robbie's shoulder.

'That's Jess, Billy's older brother. He must have finished his time at that school. What's he got there?'

They watched Jess open the door and drag a gunnysack inside. He came out with something in his hand. Robbie gasped – he was holding a crossbow! He disappeared with it and came back holding a blue guitar. Robbie blinked; no one but Chris had a guitar like that. They dodged down below the windowsill, afraid of being seen.

'What's he doin' with my guitar?' said Chris.

Downstairs Jacky, Chris's mother was feeding the baby. She called up to the boys, 'Come on down, let's have some tea.'

'Don't tell her,' said Chris. 'She'll worry, me ma. We can't afford a new one. She scrimped for months to get me that one.'

'I saw you put it behind the easels in the cellar,' said

Robbie. 'So Jess must've got in there. It was *him* you saw up at the window. He's stalking us.'

The Christmas play was to be a musical, *Guys and Dolls*. Sue invited would-be actors and singers to come back to the hall after school and show what they could do.

Robbie and the twins gave each other the thumbs up and Maddy could already see herself as Cora, the leading lady, but Chris wasn't interested.

They were gathered in the cellar after lunch, trying to persuade him, when Sue came down the stone steps with Surid, the school bursar, and stepped into their world. She stood surveying the dusty scene.

The boys and Maddy were sitting round a wooden table splashed with paint in every colour, playing cards. Sue approached and looked down at the table.

'It's called Shady Sneaks,' said Robbie, looking embarrassed. 'My cousin Jeff invented it.'

'What sort of name is that?' said Sue. Robbie wasn't sure but he thought she was hiding a smile. 'By the way, some things have gone missing from this room. We're looking for our recording equipment and the school video camera – the whole lot's gone missing. We were hoping to film the insects you're making. I don't suppose you've seen anything suspicious?'

'You did, didn't you, Chris?' said Charlie.

'I saw someone outside that window up there,' said Chris, pointing. 'And my guitar's gone missin' and I bet I know where to find it.'

Robbie pictured Jess Dodds creeping across that yard with a heavy bag.

'We're not being funny, I think we could find out for you,' he said.

Surid chuckled, cool and dismissive. 'I think you'd better leave that to us,' he said.

'As if,' muttered Chris.

Surid looked at him unpleasantly. 'Don't you children get involved in this, please, it's not a game.' He shook his forefinger at them. 'I mean it, you could be in serious trouble if you meddle in this.'

He and Sue turned and went back up the stone steps.

'But we're already involved,' said Robbie when they were out of earshot, 'and what about Chris's guitar?'

When I got home today with Chris, to do our homework, Mum and Aunt Mari were having glasses of sherry, left over from Dad's funeral. They were all shaken up because there was a big dead seagull in the garden and they said someone had shot it off the roof with a metal bolt while they were sitting out there. Sandy had come over and we went out to the field with Skywalker but we couldn't see anyone. We buried the poor gull in the field. It was huge. I want to find out what's going on.

After tea we went up to the woods, near my hideout, where Mum said they'd seen a boy earlier, killing rabbits. My guess is it's Jess Dodds. It's got to be him. And Jess is dead scary, everyone says so.

Chris is dying to get his guitar back, but we don't want to get shot. I felt safe with Billy Dodds out of the way, but now Jess is around instead. What if Jess is watching us, and wanting to get his dog back? I need to work out how to get rid of him.

It was common knowledge that the Dodds family lived off the money they made from stolen electrical goods and exotic animals, like monkeys, snakes and spiders. Billy Dodds' locker had been overflowing with the many things he'd nicked from other boys at school. It looked like Jess was the same. Light-fingered. It seemed a coincidence, though, that Jess Dodds had shot a gull from Robbie's roof, and been snooping around his school. It felt personal. Maybe Jess blamed Robbie in some way for what happened to his brother. After all, it was *his* bicycle chain that Mr Burton had been looking for when he'd found all the stolen goods in Dodds' locker. Or maybe he blamed Robbie for the police getting involved with his mum and her animal trade.

Robbie decided to lure him back to the school cellars. They could try leaving something valuable out on the table. Jess would want to grab it, especially if it was Robbie's best treasure, his binoculars. If he was looking for revenge, he'd want to take something that belonged to him, especially if it was a prized possession.

He suspected Jess had got in through the high window and lowered himself down. And if Jess was busy breaking into the school he couldn't shoot at them with his crossbow while they sneaked into the privy and grabbed the guitar and the other stuff.

For the plan to work, Robbie needed to keep in touch with someone at the school. He knew that Maddy had a phone, and she liked being one of the gang.

When Robbie told her the plan she thought for a moment and then said she'd ask Flipper to lend them his phone.

Robbie didn't have much of an idea how to work it. Flipper showed him the ropes, and Robbie slid it into his jacket pocket.

Robbie and Chris went to the sick bay complaining of sore throats, hoping to persuade the matron to let them off sick.

She looked down their throats and saw nothing wrong, but she let them off anyway.

'Fine, off with yous, I can see you two new lads need a little break,' she said.

They cycled back to Chris's, said hello to Jacky and went upstairs. Sitting by the bedroom window, they watched the Dodds' house. It was lunch time. Above the rows of houses, soft loose clouds were drifting together and forming ragged shapes. In the gaps between them, a weak milky sun struggled to break through as they waited for Jess to come out into his yard.

Chris yawned. 'This is a right waste of time,' he said. As he turned away from the window Robbie let out a yelp. There was Dodds' brother, like a rat, slipping through the yard, heading for the privy.

In a flash they were downstairs, out of the door and over the road. They stopped on the pavement right by the fence of the Dodds' yard.

'I'm going on a boat trip,' said Chris loudly. 'Can I borrow those posh binoculars of yours? They look cracker. I know you don't like parting with them, but there might be whales.'

'I've gone and left them in the cellar room at school,' said Robbie. 'I'll pick them up tomorrow and you can have them, as long as you look after them. They're brilliant, I'll bust your head if you go and lose them.'

They walked on by, hoping Jess had heard. At the end of the block they hid behind a car and watched to see whether he took the bait. When they saw that he was hopping on to a moped, Robbie texted Maddy.

'Jess has left. He's on a moped. He could be there soon.'

'OK,' replied Maddy. 'I'll let you know what happens.'

Jess Dodds is dangerous and he may be back any minute – he could've just gone to the corner shop. But I'm hoping he's gone after my binoculars. Maddy's our spy. When she says he's at school, we'll go and get the guitar back from the yard. We can be in and out again dead quick. This fancy phone's buzzing. It's Maddy. He's there!

Chris and Robbie sprinted across the road. They helped each other over the gate and crept across the filthy yard, past sagging cages and a couple of drooping, bedraggled peacocks. They opened the door of the privy and stepped inside. A mound on the floor looked as if it could be the gunnysack. There was a gust of wind and the door slammed shut leaving them in thick darkness. Flipper had shown Robbie the torch on his phone. He fumbled to switch it on, and then jumped back, shouting, 'Watch out!'

In the corner was coiled a yellowish snake.

A scene came into his mind, complete and vivid. He remembered the woman in black arriving at the twins' family party, pretending to be Mrs Marvella, a children's entertainer. He could picture her as she scooped a beautiful, pale snake out of a basket for the children to play with. This snake looked to be the same species; he was pretty sure it wouldn't hurt a fly.

He shouted with relief, 'It's all right, Chris. That snake's harmless.'

The snake, watchful, eyed them malevolently. The boys grabbed the sack and shone the torch round to see if there was anything else. Behind the reptile there was a glint – the crossbow.

'Let's throw it in the canal,' said Chris, who was keeping a wary eye on the recumbent snake as it flickered its tongue at him.

'No, let's just get out quick. We're done for if he comes back and finds us,' said Robbie. 'Have you found your guitar?'

'Yes, it's here, with the filming stuff. We'd better go.'

They grabbed the sack and guitar and left. As soon as they were safely inside Chris's house, they rang Maddy.

She sounded excited.

'Hey, get this,' she said. 'I reported seeing someone suspicious at the window of the cellar, but when Surid went to challenge him, he ran off. He got away. He left a rope hanging from the window. He's on a moped. And he had your binoculars round his neck.'

'Please get someone to come over here, Maddy. We've got the school's filming stuff,' said Robbie, urgently. He gave Chris's address.

'I'll tell Surid now,' said Maddy.

'Thanks.'

'At your service, oh great detective,' said Maddy in a theatrical voice, clearly enjoying the drama.

'Thanks, Maddy, tell him to hurry.'

They waited at the window, peering anxiously across the road. No sign of Jess yet.

Surid pulled up outside in a big four-by-four and they went out to hand over the sack. Surid raised his eyebrows and scowled at them.

'Now, where did you find this stuff? What else was there?'

Robbie and Chris had thought he'd be pleased. Reluctantly, they told him what they'd done. Robbie said there was a crossbow and that he was pretty sure Jess had shot at Robbie's house with it. Surid's face set hard. Robbie didn't like his stony expression so he decided not to say any more.

'You must listen to me,' he said. 'You boys must go inside your house and stay there. Tell your mother not to open the door or go out.'

'What about getting my binoculars back?' said Robbie anxiously. 'I use them a lot.'

But Surid was speaking to someone on the phone.

Nodding his head, he said, 'Sure thing, will do. I'll just make sure the boys are out of the way.'

They were bundled into the house. Watching from the upstairs window they saw Surid trying to get into the yard. But the gate was still locked. Minutes later a police van came hurtling round the corner. At the same moment a moped appeared at the other end of the street. Robbie's pulse skittered as he watched Jess spot the cops and swerve round, skidding on the tarmac.

'Oh God, don't let him get away,' he prayed under his breath.

Behind Jess a large armoured four-by-four with a flashing blue light drove up, blocking his path. Jess dropped the bike and looked round wildly. For a moment it looked as though he was ready to run, but Robbie could see that Jess was trapped.

CHAPTER 26
The dragon's den

Robbie decided to do some research in the library at the arts centre. The rain was tipping down outside. By the time he arrived he was like a drowned rat.

Julie, clad in a yellow dress with large red pineapples on it, came out of her office. Robbie stood before her, his sopping windcheater dripping on the floor.

'You're drenched,' she said sympathetically, removing his jacket and putting it on a peg in the hall. Robbie explained that he'd come to look for a book on reptiles. He told Julie about Miss Bryony's lesson and how fascinating it'd been.

'My boss has masses of books on snakes in his office,' said Julie. 'He must be fascinated too. He's out this morning. Why don't you go up there and have a quick look?' She put her finger to her lips. 'Don't tell anyone I let you.'

Robbie couldn't believe his luck. He could find out all Rory O'Connor's secrets. A detective needed a bit of luck sometimes.

His eyes were keenly on the lookout as he bounded into the dragon's den. For a few moments he just sat in the swivel chair, enjoying spinning round and trying to decide what to do now he was here. What was he on the lookout for? This was enemy territory so he had to be careful. Suppose the guy came back?

I'm in Rory O'Connor's office and now I can do some real detective work. I've looked at the painting of the snake and cased the joint for a safe place to hide. Actually, there isn't anywhere much. I suppose I could get behind the curtain. I'd better get on with what I've come for.

There are loads of bookshelves. They have glass doors but they aren't locked. I'm going to look up Mrs Dodds' yellow snake first. I remember what Miss Bryony said. There are golden snakes on Snake Island. Like in my dream. They're called lanceheads. Why does Rory O'Connor have a picture of one over his fireplace, and one on his notebook? And all these books on snakes. This is like a puzzle and I need to solve it.

I might need this: *Venomous Snakes of the World*. And here's one called *Venom: Secrets of Nature's Deadliest Weapon*.

Robbie turned his head towards the door, listening. Sure enough, he heard light footsteps hurrying up the stairs. He grabbed the books he'd picked out and jumped behind the curtain.

The footsteps came into the room and Robbie could hear shuffling noises, like papers being handled. Moments later, more footsteps came through the door. Robbie didn't dare move to see what was going on, but he knew soon enough.

'Oh, there you are. I was looking for you. There's no one looking after the reception desk. Forgive me, but just what *are* you doing in my room, Julie?'

Robbie knew that voice: it was Rory O'Connor all right.

'Just tidying your desk, Rory, is that all right?'

'Well, I'd rather do it myself if you don't mind. Some of those papers are very confidential.'

'Of course,' said Julie, sounding like sweetness itself. 'Oh, and there's something I need to show you, down in the library, something I thought would interest you. I can take you down now if you like.'

Rory said nothing as two sets of footsteps left the room and headed down the stairs.

Robbie held on to the books and lifted a couple of documents from the table for good measure. He had time to hide in the lavatory and waited there until he heard O'Connor's footsteps mount the stairs once more. The office door slammed shut.

Grabbing his moment, he tiptoed along the corridor and down the stairs. Then he ran for it, whispering, 'Thanks, Julie, you were ace,' as he shot past her desk, seizing his sodden jacket, which he hoped had not been spotted by O'Connor.

'The tips of your trainers were sticking out from under the curtain!' hissed Julie as he sped away to safety.

The following day he, Maddy and the twins sat down together in the old art room with cans of red lemonade and the books and documents from O'Connor's room. Elbows on the table and heads propped on hands, they got to work.

'This one's boring, it's about snake venom and its chemical composition. Different types of snake have different venoms. It says here it's used for medical research,' said Charlie.

'This is all stuff about pit vipers,' said Harry, 'and the

number of people killed every year by snake bites. Between 81,000 and 138,000, it says on the back cover. Over a million people are bitten by poisonous snakes each year, mostly in Africa, and tens of thousands in South America. It says here that even if you *survive* a bite, if you aren't treated quickly with an antidote your limb can turn black and has to be amputated.'

'My book says a golden lancehead, which is a very special and rare pit viper, has venom that's lethal, but is also used for medicine and is worth a fortune, $30,000. How much is a dollar worth?'

'Not sure,' said Maddy, 'but it must be heaps of money.'

'So how can Mrs Dodds afford to buy a snake worth all that money?' said Robbie.

'Do you remember her snake from our party?' said Charlie.

Robbie jumped up, knocking over his chair.

'Of course! That tiger and the poor monkey. Mrs Dodds must be getting all her animals from somewhere. Someone's smuggling in dangerous wild animals and selling the snakes for their venom. Maybe Mrs Dodds gets the odd snake that doesn't have venom.'

They looked at each other.

'So you think the kidnappers were smuggling snakes?' said Harry. 'That was dead risky.'

'There must be a place somewhere where they remove the venom. That's an even more dangerous job than smuggling,' said Robbie.

'Who's the boss of the operation, though?' said Maddy, sending them all into quiet thoughtfulness.

They continued their reading. After a couple of minutes, Robbie jumped up, flourishing an official-looking letter.

'Listen to this. It's from a medical laboratory in Westport in England and it's asking about an order for ten pit vipers. Guess where I found it?'

'Where?'

'Where did you find it?'

Robbie's voice dropped to a whisper. 'Same place I got these books from. Rory O'Connor's office.'

CHAPTER 27

Friend or foe?

Robbie went to the woods that evening after school and sat down under his tree. The leaves above murmured and rustled in the breeze and a blackbird was blithely singing.

He got out a packet of crisps and started to eat them absent-mindedly. He needed to get things clear.

He didn't much want to tell Brendan Bentham about his discovery. After all, he'd seen Brendan in Rory O'Connor's office. Perhaps they were working together. Was that why they never found the contraband on the trawler? Perhaps the two old men had been warned just in time and had thrown the snakes and the rest of the stuff overboard or something.

But Brendan had taken Robbie and the twins with him on that mission, and when they'd got to the bunker Terry and the old men were still there, on board the trawler, so they couldn't have been tipped off.

In any case Robbie liked Brendan, and so did Aunt Mari, so he didn't want to think he was crooked. Even so, he felt he couldn't really trust anyone at this point; he had to think about possible suspects and not leave anyone out. His hand reached into an empty packet. He'd eaten the whole bag of crisps without noticing. He lay on his stomach and tried to concentrate.

Who else could be involved? There was Mrs Dodds.

Although Jess had been arrested, Mrs Dodds had been allowed out. But she didn't seem terribly rich, so how could she be the one masterminding the smuggling of illegal animals? He started wondering how Skywalker had come into her hands.

Why did Mrs Dodds even want Skywalker? She didn't deserve to own that cool dog, she practically starved him. And he's so special. Dogs are amazing. They have super senses. He can smell things and hear things no human being can smell or hear. I wonder if Sky could help me find out what happened to the cargo that night. If I could take Sky to the bunker to look for clues – traces of animals or something – I might be able to solve the mystery. If I'm going to prove someone is smuggling live creatures, I need a lead to find the boss of the ring. Then I can get him in handcuffs. It would be awful if it was Brendan.

First, I need to get my binoculars back from Surid. I saw him talking to the police and he got them to hand them over, which was good. I suppose he must've been listening when I said I wanted them back. Funny, I didn't think he was. But then he went round the back of Mrs Dodds' house and I didn't see what he did with them after that.

Robbie knocked on the bursar's door. He heard Surid's voice saying, 'Just a moment.' A couple of minutes passed slowly by; there was definitely something about standing outside the closed door that made Robbie uncomfortable. He tried to be his detective self and listen to what was going on, but all he could hear was that Surid sounded cross. Finally, he heard the bursar saying goodbye to someone, and a click that sounded like him putting down the phone. 'Enter,' he called out. Robbie went into a room as neat as a hospital ward, and as sparse. No hint of his character to be found. No carelessly scattered papers *here*.

'Well, here comes trouble,' said Surid, attempting to be jovial. But his face was pale and waxy. He had the look of someone who'd been up all night. 'What can I do for you, Robbie?'

Robbie came straight to the point. 'I'd like my binoculars back, please.'

'And what do you use them for, may I ask?' said Surid, pushing his reading glasses up on to his head and looking weary. Were his large brown eyes kind? Robbie wasn't so sure.

'I like birdwatching,' said Robbie. Surid didn't actually need to know anything else.

'And how did you find our filming equipment?' Robbie realised he was going to be interrogated. He rather wished he hadn't come; he wished he'd asked Sue to get them back for him.

'Just hanging out with Chris, who lives opposite the Dodds' yard,' he said, raising his eyebrows and smiling a bit, in order to look as candid as possible.

'And what else did you see?'

'Nothing much,' he said.

'There must have been something?' insisted Surid.

'No,' said Robbie, pretending to think, 'I can't remember seeing anything else except the crossbow.'

Surid leaned back in his chair and seemed to be thinking aloud. 'I thought you, above everyone, might have noticed something.' He looked at Robbie's face keenly. 'You seem to be quite able to put two and two together.' He pulled himself up. 'Right,' he said, his expression a picture of fatherly concern, 'well, don't do any more interfering. The police have everything in hand. And look after these, don't leave them lying about,' he said, handing over the binoculars.

His smile looked almost real.

'We don't want you children getting mixed up in this sort of thing, do we? Off you go.'

Robbie closed the door behind him and let out a deep breath.

CHAPTER 28

The insect parade

On top of Poets' Mound a beacon flared in the dark, visible for miles around. A strongly built bonfire sparked and leaped and crackled as it caught hold, dry wood sending a twisting column of smoke into the starry night sky. A sound recording of crickets, rustling leaves, whooping monkeys and jungle birds was drifting out from a loudspeaker. Down below, the carnival of luminous insects was getting ready to climb to the top to be greeted by parents, music and a barbecue supper, provided by the school but cooked by the upper-school students. Sue was at the ready, with a cameraman filming the whole thing.

The lower-school children had built their pantomime insects from fresh willow wands soaked in water, and a special kind of model-aeroplane paper, durable yet light, glued firmly on to the willow structures. The faces of the ants, grasshoppers, butterflies and bees, with eyes painted on, were made with papier mâché. Underneath were struts to hold the structures together and wands to hold them up with.

The children were getting inside with their torches, ready to start the procession. Someone was having trouble with their dragonfly, its fragile wings dipping and dragging on the grass. Robbie and the twins – hot, red in the face, and agitated inside their giant ant – were discovering that it was extremely hard to see where they were going now it was dark. The eyeholes, which had seemed fine to Charlie in daylight, were definitely too small.

Robbie got out from underneath the construction.

'I'll run down and get some scissors,' he said to the twins. 'We've still got a few minutes.'

He set off for the school. The old house lay quiet. Everyone was out for the carnival. Robbie entered by the kitchens, where cookers, tables of steel and hanging pots were eerily gleaming. He hunted for scissors but couldn't find any.

Along the corridor next to the kitchen were the science labs.

'Bound to be scissors in there,' he said to himself.

But this part of the school was for the A-level students only, out of bounds to him. Like a good detective, he had a torch on him, so at least he wouldn't have to risk putting the lights on. He moved quietly, sniffing a scent – some chemical he couldn't quite place. Then it came back to him; the funeral parlour had smelled like this when he'd visited his dad. He shuddered.

All was still in the deserted lab. It had large windows and in the distance he could see the bonfire, which was lighting the room with the faintest glow. Rows of glass specimen bottles reflected the distant flames in miniature. A tap dripped. Robbie moved silently as he looked for scissors on the worktops. On the second bench, he found the perfect pair and quickly picked them up.

A slight click. The door at the far end of the room opened.

Robbie ducked down and lay on his stomach under a workbench. A low table light went on at the far end of the lab. He could make out a figure, a man, bending over a workbench. What was he holding? Yes! He had a dead snake in his hand. Just visible in the pool of light from the lamp, the man picked up a large glass jar. Robbie heard liquid being poured, smelled again that powerful whiff of embalming fluid, and saw the snake, a black coil in the clear liquid, as it dropped into the jar. The man closed the lid and placed it alongside the row of glass jars on the shelf. He got out his phone and sat down.

'O'Connor? It's Surid. Do you want the good news or the bad news?' A pause. 'I've finally got the second shipment. It's not been easy with Mrs Dodds out of action, but she's out and about again now.'

Robbie strained but he couldn't hear what O'Connor was saying at the other end.

'Some of the best specimens haven't survived, but the contact at Westport will still take whatever we've got, as long as the venom is intact. So go and make sure they're ready to go. And make sure the transport is here at the stables tomorrow at midday.'

Surid stood up. Robbie, lying prone on the lino, flattened himself, shrinking into the deep black shadow where the wall met the floor. The crow-like silhouette of the bursar, shoulders up, seemed to be looking about. Robbie held his breath. Surid appeared to find nothing to make him suspicious and left.

Robbie, trembling, found he was holding the scissors tightly in his hand and remembered what they were for. Rolling out from beneath the bench, he stood listening. No sound. Stealthily, he made his getaway, slipping out through the dark kitchens.

Luck was on his side. Weak with relief, he managed to get back to the twins just in time. He handed over the scissors and Charlie hacked at the ant's head to make larger eyeholes. Then off they went. Robbie, hunched up in the belly of the ant, felt for a moment cocooned from reality, as if none of it had happened, as they followed the column of glowing, fairylike creatures winding slowly up Poet's Mound towards the beacon. The loudspeaker played Saint-Saëns' *Carnival of the Animals* and when the last of the insects, a dragonfly with trailing wings, reached the top, there was a burst of applause from the parents and children waiting by the bonfire.

Surid was already there, standing at Sue's elbow.

Bats swirled and looped overhead in the darkness. Drinks were poured amid loud chatter. Robbie went and said hello to his mum and Aunt Mari, who said Brendan was late as usual, but on his way.

Maddy and the twins came over and the four of them went into a huddle. Robbie summed up the situation succinctly, as a good detective should. The trouble was, what to do about it? Could they sort this out themselves? Brendan would arrive at the bonfire party any minute and they could easily hand over to him. On the one hand they felt they *ought* to tell, but on the other, did they *want* to tell? Remembering the fun they'd at the Ifflick Bar, they came to a conclusion of sorts. Not to tell *all*, but to ask Brendan to be in the vicinity tomorrow in case he was needed.

Sitting in a circle on the ground, just out of reach of the bonfire's glow and drinking fruit punch from paper cups, Robbie and the others made a plan. When he saw Brendan, Robbie would mention the specimens he'd seen in the laboratory, explaining that he thought snakes were important in the smuggling case, and that there might possibly be fingerprints. If Brendan was in the lab, Robbie thought, he could quickly come to the stables and help out, if and when he was needed. But Robbie wanted to be there first to unmask the ringleader himself.

CHAPTER 29

Plans – do they have a life of their own?

It's easy enough to make a plan, but then you have to carry it out. That's more difficult. Things can go wrong – badly wrong, in fact.

Robbie, Maddy and the twins decided to case the stable block early the next day, with the idea of setting a tripwire. Chris couldn't come; his little sister was ailing and he was needed at home.

The four of them planned that Surid would fall over the knee-high wire and come crashing down. Then they could overwhelm him by sheer numbers. They would lock him in a loose box and get him to confess. Or just hand him over to Brendan. It was simple.

The twins had brought with them wire, screws and a screwdriver. The outstanding problem was where to put the tripwire.

Having looked round the ground floor, where the old wood-lined stables and tack room lay deserted, they mounted steep steps to the large, unused upper floor. Here the grooms and stable boys once had their quarters. A space with alcoves of peeling white-painted brick, furnished with iron bedsteads, had once been a dormitory for the lads and men working with the horses. In the living quarters was an old black stove, a line of washbasins, a defunct loo.

Now, all was covered in the filth of small decaying things that can fall from an untended roof. It was given over to spiders, rats, bats and mice. It was derelict and dusty, exuding a smell of rot. In some parts the floor had fallen away.

Robbie was hunting for signs that someone had been there, had used the place as a store or a hideout. Busy with his thoughts, he wandered to the end of the attic.

A dim light came through narrow, cobwebbed windows. In the far wall was a smallish door. He opened it and peered into the darkness. He stepped forward, instantly disturbing a number of roosting pigeons. One or two rose and flew about with a loud clattering of wings.

Switching on his torch, he realised there was no proper floor, only beams with fragile-looking sawdust boarding nailed between them.

He took a cautious step along a beam, searching for clues. He heard the twins calling him so turned to go back and, at that moment, a pigeon flew straight into his face. Its small body, hard under the warm mass of feathers, hit him like a tennis ball served at speed.

There was a moment when he thought he could save himself and get his balance back. He teetered, lurched and, with eyes shut tight and stomach griping, he toppled and fell with a crash through the boards, into a shower of pigeon droppings and dust. It was a short fall. He landed with a thump on top of something hard and metallic. Stunned and winded, he brushed the dirt from his face and eyes. He was still clutching his torch.

There was a fanlight above what looked like garage doors. Sprawled amid heaps of bird droppings and ripped boarding, he could just about see that he was on the roof of a four-by-four. He shone the torch inside it. What he saw made him throw himself off the car roof on to the floor and scramble for the door.

He threw open the doors and crawled out, looking as if he'd been caught in a bomb blast. Maddy and the twins came running over to him. He called out hoarsely, 'It's here. The evidence...'

He sat down abruptly on the ground, holding one ankle, choking on dust, unable to speak another word.

Robbie woke up in his own bed, aware of nothing but a throbbing pain in his ankle. He groaned and pulled off the bedclothes to find his left leg bandaged. He looked around, trying to remember what had happened. A pair of grey metal crutches leaned where he could reach them beside the bed.

A warm yellowish light filtered in between the curtains. What the time was, he had no idea. He remembered going into the pigeon loft and crashing down. That was it.

He called out and heard his mum's footsteps on the stairs.

'So you're awake at last,' she said, coming over to the bed. 'You've been in the wars. I'll bring you some lunch and there's a visitor who wants to see you. And don't try walking without your crutches.'

'What's wrong with my leg? It's sore. In fact, everything's sore. I'm hurting all over,' he said.

'You fractured your ankle when you fell on that car. Lucky the roof didn't give way or you'd have been in real trouble.'

She brought him a ham sandwich and a painkiller. Then he heard footsteps on the stairs. Brendan Bentham put his head round the door.

'Sorry you had such a hell of a fall. Are you ready to hear how things are going on your case?' he said.

Robbie perked up, tried to sit up and then stopped, screwing his face up in pain.

Brendan continued, 'You're a whole lot cleaner since the last time I saw you.'

'When was that?' said Robbie, through a mouthful of sandwich.

'Yesterday,' he said, 'at the stables. Thanks to you and your accident, everything was suddenly a whole lot clearer. I've been trying for months to solve this case. I'd only bits and snatches of it.'

'Surid,' said Robbie.

'Spot on, and I reckon you got there faster than me,' said Brendan. 'I got the old men locked up for kidnapping, very much thanks to you. But without evidence, apart from the submarine which was empty, I couldn't accuse them of smuggling. We took that trawler apart, but we found nothing on board except tanks of live lobsters. Likely they heard us coming and threw the cargo overboard at the last minute. But they didn't have time to get off the boat and get away.'

'So who's the ringleader?' said Robbie. 'I thought at first it was Rory O'Connor.'

'You caught on all right, Robbie. It was the two of them. They're in it together. All that time Mari and I were keeping our relationship low-key while the investigation was ongoing, and it turns out that I'd been using the office of one of the ringleaders the whole time!'

'So *that's* why Aunt Mari was so secretive about you?' asked Robbie.

'Exactly,' said Bentham. 'I didn't want the smugglers knowing that a detective was in their midst. Turns out, they were supplying snakes to a laboratory in Westport. We found six lethal snakes inside that Range Rover you fell on. Maddy came and told me you'd fallen. I was in the science lab looking at the jars of specimens. And well done. Surid's fingerprints were all over those jars.'

Robbie smiled at Brendan. 'I was hot on their heels, wasn't I?'

'You were, Robbie, you surely were. Though how you did it, I can't say! A few of the snakes must have died – terrible when you think someone had risked their life to capture them, and I believe some are protected too. Surid had found a way of disposing of the dead ones, by turning them into specimens for the students.'

'What did Rory O'Connor have to do with it?' said Robbie.

'O'Connor had an abiding interest in snakes and a friend

working at the lab. They needed pit vipers and it was getting harder to obtain them. He recruited Surid to get them. Apparently he's got a lot of contacts in Brazil, where most of the snakes come from. And believe it or not, Mrs Dodds is part of it.' Brendan chuckled. 'A weak link at that. She takes some of the duds, ones without venom. The lab, of course, can't use them. Some are rare and worth tens of thousands of pounds and those he sells on the black market. O'Connor sees to transferring the venomous ones to the lab.'

'O'Connor, Surid and Mrs Dodds?' said Robbie. 'No wonder Surid didn't seem pleased when he learned we'd found the stolen school camera in the Dodds' yard! But I thought medical labs were a good thing?' said Robbie, who was starting to yawn openly, in spite of himself. 'They help people, don't they?'

'Absolutely they do. They've saved thousands of lives. They're using the venom to make antidotes for bites and some is stored and used for research. They never knew the snakes came illegally. We shan't go after the lab. Our task is to stop the smuggling, and now we have enough evidence to make sure O'Connor and Surid don't do anything like this again for a *very* long time.'

Robbie lay curled up, round as a shell, and felt his eyes closing. The warm bed, the paracetamol and the sandwich had soothed his aching body and he drifted off.

CHAPTER 30

No smoke without fire

The day started hazy, but now a warm sun was breaking through. Robbie and his mum joined Fay and the twins and drove to the fishing quays. Sandy was already stripped to the waist as he prepared the *Santa Fay* for the outing – hosing it down, sorting out life jackets and a cushion or two, a canvas cover for the stern deck.

Robbie thought Sandy seemed nervous. He was looking anxiously along the quay.

'Here we are!' shouted Robbie, as they struggled along carrying bags and parasols and all sorts of stuff. Rose walked along talking and laughing with Fay, who was wrestling with several large bags. Robbie had a bright red plastic cool box and the twins were carrying flippers and snorkels.

Sandy's face changed as he saw them approaching the *Santa Fay*. He jumped out of the boat, smiling as he went to meet them.

'Here we are!' called Rose. 'We've hardly brought anything with us at all. I hope it's OK, there's quite a few of us.'

'Let me help. That looks heavy,' he said, taking the bags from Robbie's mum.

'It's all got to be eaten,' said Rose. 'Fay's cooked enough for an army. Fay, have you met Sandy Sitwell? Well, of course, for God's sake, you've heard him singing! Isn't he just something?'

Robbie's leg was still in a special boot, designed to allow his ankle to heal. He had his binoculars round his neck, in case there might be dolphins, or even whales. He watched his mum, who looked relaxed in her blue cotton dress and sun hat, chattering away. He liked seeing her looking so happy. It all seemed to be going well.

'Where's Skywalker, Sandy?' he asked.

'Sorry, Robbie. He's had to stay home today. That dog's walking the legs right off me,' said Sandy. 'He's so fit now we could train him to run.'

'Doesn't he know how to run?' said Harry.

'Run races, Harry, at the track. He's a working dog and he loves to run. I'm thinking he could be a winner,' said Sandy. 'Now! We've got the tide, who wants to get on board?'

There was a good deal of chaos, sorting out the muddle of bags, flippers and parasols. Then, with a good deal of teasing, everybody bridged the lurching gap between stone quay and moving boat. A fishing boat isn't the easiest thing to get on to. They jumped up, tottering, stumbling and tripping over. Sandy helped Robbie, the others managed somehow, and there was no falling in.

They thrummed out of the harbour and started to pick up speed. Robbie and the twins were watching for whales; there were sometimes minkes in the North Channel. Sandy handed life jackets to the boys and made sure they put them on the right way up. The twins in their baseball caps soon gave up on whale-watching and went to the cabin to help Sandy pilot the boat.

The light was shimmering on the water and seagulls, floating above them, stayed with them in case fishing was about to start. Fay and Rose were given a couple of old deckchairs and settled themselves on the stern deck.

The two of them, now wearing sunglasses, were clearly enjoying each other's company. The sun shone on a perfect, tranquil bay. The quays were already far away and hazy.

There was a shout from Robbie. He ran forwards to give Sandy his binoculars.

'Sandy, look over there, I think it's a boat. I can see smoke.'

They all went to the rail to see what was happening. In the distance they could see smoke low on the water. Sandy turned the wheel and headed towards it. In a few minutes they were closing in.

As they approached, they could just see two figures on board, partly obscured by the dense smoke. They were putting on life jackets and seemed to be arguing. One of them, the smaller man, jumped overboard.

Robbie looked through his binoculars again. The taller figure was struggling with a fire extinguisher, which didn't appear to be working.

'Sandy, it's Jeff!' shouted Robbie.

And the boat was the *Blue Fairy*! And Robbie began to suspect he knew who the smaller figure in the water was.

'Better get off there fast!' yelled Sandy to Jeff as he carefully approached the swimmer through the smoky murk. And sure enough, it was an exhausted Windy Wake they fished out of the water, his tight curls dripping, his face white. He lay on his back on the steel deck, water streaming everywhere.

'He promised he was right behind me,' he panted. 'The bloody thing's going to explode any second. He's only just bought it and he wants to save it. Get him out of there!'

'Jeff! Jeff! Can you hear me? It's Robbie. When I was on the *Blue Fairy*, I saw another fire extinguisher. Look under the galley table. I hit my head on it.'

A moment later there was a shout from Jeff. 'Got it!'

There was a hiss as the fire extinguisher started to spout foam. The smoke was thicker, yellowish-brown now, smelling of oil and billowing everywhere in a cloud, blocking out the sun and drifting up into the clear air above.

They were all in a row, gripping the rail as they strained to see. They could hear Jeff coughing, but couldn't see much in the fog.

'Get out now, Jeff!' called Rose. 'Quick! Fast as you can.'

There was a splash and they waited, breathless.

In the gap between the two boats, black smears over his face, Jeff came swimming towards them.

'I've put it out, I think,' he gasped as he reached the *Santa Fay*. They managed to heave him up on to the deck.

'Jeff!' said Windy. 'Thank God, I thought you were going to die.'

'It's all right, I'm fine,' said Jeff, just before he lost consciousness.

Everyone has gone home now. We had a very exciting

time. No one was hurt, although Jeff and Windy both have headaches and they're still coughing. It was such a narrow escape. Jeff passed out. Windy was so worried. But then he woke up, and Windy could see he was going to be all right. He started jumping all over the place. He's such a show-off. Then he said, 'At least I'll have something to tell the grandchildren!'

I thought at first he was confused after breathing in all that smoke. People do sometimes start saying weird things when they've been hit on the head or in a dangerous situation. Then Jeff came up and put his arm around Windy and said, 'All right, Dad?'

They'd kept it all a secret, but now we all know.

Jeff says he started trying to find his real father and mother last year and he found Windy, which was a big surprise, and he discovered his mother was a dancer too! She lives in California. When Windy left for Canada he didn't know he was going to be a dad. He says she never told him.

Everyone knew Jeff was adopted. But he's always called Martin Dad. Now he has two dads. He's so lucky. I suppose that was why Windy was being so nice to Jeff, buying him tickets and taking him out for drinks. The Ifflick Bar was a secret place to meet if you didn't want your family to know. Jeff didn't know how his parents would feel and thought they might be upset. He's told them now and they're happy for him.

We saved the *Blue Fairy* but she looks awful, all black.

The engine was on fire and it was about to blow up, but Jeff saved it. So Sandy towed it behind the *Santa Fay* back to port. We had our picnic there on the fishing quays while Windy took Jeff off to the hospital to be checked over. The boat will need a lot of work done to it, Jeff says. Maybe I can help him.

CHAPTER 31

The green garden

Robbie was in the woods, under his oak tree. Above his den the light was golden-green, the air buzzing with insects. Now and then a squirrel ran along a branch over his head.

It was the start of the summer holidays. Robbie, enjoying the feeling of freedom, reflected that the bad memory of his tormentor, Dodds, had faded. When he did remember him, he said to himself, 'Just imagine having a mother like that...' He even felt some sympathy for him. But he hadn't forgiven him completely for making his life such a misery.

Sandy had gone to visit the fearsome Mrs Dodds, who'd again managed to escape jail somehow – although Bentham had told Robbie that he'd taken measures to ensure she wouldn't be keeping animals again. Sandy pretended he'd found Skywalker wandering the streets and taken him in. He offered Mrs Dodds £50 and eventually paid her £100 for Skywalker. Luckily, she hadn't seen the dog as he looks now, a strong, lithe, muscled animal, glimmering white as a pearl, with dark gracious eyes. If she had, she'd certainly have asked for more.

Thank goodness his mum was happy again and had time for teasing Robbie and trying to help a bit with his homework, although he was well ahead of her most of the time. He'd decided that as well as being a detective and a singer, he wanted to be a vet and help look after animals that were badly treated. Finding out what was wrong with them would be interesting, and having seen some animals suffering, he wanted to do something about it. But now it was the holidays and he was happily ensconced in the woods.

I'm under my oak tree, looking at the back of our house through my binoculars. I can see Mum on her own, sitting in the kitchen. The garden is full of tall grass and weeds. Mum says it's like a jungle. My dad used to mow the grass and look after it, but no one does it now.

Now Mum has gone out of sight. OK, now she's coming back and it looks as if she's filling the kettle.

I'm here to look for a good spot for our tent. I'm going to camp out tonight with Chris and the twins. Maddy's mum doesn't want her to come, but maybe she can persuade her. Jeff's coming over to cook supper with us, because Mum is going out singing with Sandy tonight.

We're going to cook beans on the camping stove and roll them up in bread, like we did in the boat shed. We could cook sausages too. I think we can camp right here in the field. We don't need to hide.

Now there's someone coming out of my house into the garden. It's Sandy, with Skywalker! Sky is looking happy, he's the best dog ever.

Sandy is hacking at the weeds with something and clearing a space in the middle of the garden. Mum's coming out in her shorts with mugs of tea. She's putting the mugs down on the old wooden table. I'd better not spy on them, I don't think they'd like it. But they're moving towards each other.

Robbie put the binoculars down and watched from the woods as the pearly white greyhound explored the small green wilderness. He was happy to see two figures coming together in the heart of the garden and embracing for what seemed like a long, long time.

Published in the UK by Universe
an imprint of Unicorn Publishing Group, 2022
Charleston Studio
Meadow Business Centre
Lewes BN8 5RW

www.unicornpublishing.org

10 9 8 7 6 5 4 3 2 1

ISBN 978-1-914414-53-4

Cover design and illustration by Caroline Conran
Typeset by Vivian Head

Printed in the UK